The Caroline Affair

The Caroline Affair

C. H. Gibbs-Smith

1954

New York · The Viking Press

Library of Congress catalog card number: 54-6423

PRINTED IN U. S. A. BY THE COLONIAL PRESS INC.

"I always wonder, at Paul's parties, how many of the guests are his patients—past or present."

And the answer from Henry Barclay, who had his back to me. "Oh, probably quite a few from the past, I expect; psychiatrists often keep up with their successful cases, and I should think Paul has more than his share of successes."

"If you are talking about me, Henry," I said as I came up, "you are a flatterer. I have just as many failures as the next man."

"What goes to make most of the failures, Paul?" This was from Henry's wife, Sandra.

I was just about to reply that it was about fifty-fifty between my professional incompetence and the patient's unwillingness or inability to cooperate, when Sarah tapped me gently on the arm from behind and said, "Mr. Paul, you are wanted on the telephone; I've put it through to the library." So with an apology I turned and followed her through the pleasant hubbub. After me trailed Sandra's voice. "Poor Paul, his neurotics can't even let him alone on party nights."

As I followed Sarah out of the room I was wondering if Sandra Barclay would ever discover that Henry, her faithful and able husband, had once been one of my patients—and a successful one, at that.

I knew from the way Sarah spoke that this telephone call

was what we referred to colloquially as "police business." Sarah also knew that within this category a call from Sir George Cayley was top priority, and that I had to be reached immediately, wherever I was and whatever I was doing. Entering the library, I noticed that she had carried out the necessary routine for these calls. She had pressed down the switch which isolated the telephone from the other extensions in the flat, and had pushed home the "scrambler" button on the instrument itself.

I sat on the side of my deep armchair and picked up the receiver. "Paul Harvard here."

"Paul, it's George. I'm sorry to interrupt your party, but something rather urgent has come up. How soon can you see me without upsetting things too much?"

"Straight away if necessary. I can get Sarah to make my apologies as people start looking for me, and Diana will be a good hostess. But can you send a car? Alfred is helping with the party."

"Yes, I'll send Martin. I think it had better be now, as I don't know quite what to do. I've got a casualty on my hands —a very valuable one—and I think you ought to bring some sedatives. She's with me at Scotland Yard, and in rather bad shape."

I told him I would be prepared, and hung up. I then sent for Sarah, and when that placid member of my household appeared I asked her to shut the door behind her. "Sarah, Sir George wants to see me at once—he's sending Martin, so we needn't bother Alfred. Would you go and find Mrs. Plunkett and tell her I've been called away on a case and would she please act as hostess where necessary. Then if you stand near the door you can make my apologies if you see anyone about to leave who seems to be looking for me. I have no idea when I shall be back, so don't wait up."

Dear Sarah, I thought as I put some things in a bag and prepared to leave. How many thousands of bachelors must pray for such a maternal and efficient person to look after them. She had grown up with our family and insisted on the non-medical "Mister" where I was concerned. I knew perfectly well that she would be sitting up for me, no matter what time I returned; but we always kept to the familiar form of words in such cases.

I went down in the lift and sat waiting in the hotel lounge. It was then that I idly speculated as to what had happened to put George Cayley out of his usually profound composure; for he was unquestionably put out. His voice had something odd that one did not often hear in it, a mixed note of solicitude and anxiety. And it was a woman he had on his hands—a "valuable casualty" he had called her. But I had had to see so many curious people in my work for him that I dismissed the whole business from my mind and spent the time until my arrival at Scotland Yard in idly speculating about the symbolism of a Blake drawing which a friend of mine had shown me that morning, and about which he was writing a learned article.

I have always retained an affection for the ugly buildings of Scotland Yard—it is perhaps the romanticism of my half-American parentage—and it was an old friend who greeted me after I had pushed open the shabby swing doors. He was Sergeant Holmes (no doubt his juniors called him Sherlock) and he grinned when he saw who it was.

"Sir George has gone to the Deputy Commissioner's office, Dr. Harvard, and he'd like you to go straight up."

3

"Thank you, Holmes," I said. "And how are the sweet peas?"

"Still having trouble with the neighbour, Doctor; he says I'm impeding the view from his ground-floor window with my poles!"

It was Holmes, one of the acknowledged sweet-pea authorities in the country and a fellow bachelor, who had once explained me to a new colleague of his—and was overheard by our Alfred—as "a kind of a Yankee nerve specialist who's called in for advice on some of the loonies we meet up with on the job." It was as good a story as any other, and was tacitly encouraged by the authorities.

I came out of the lift, turned to the left, and walked slowly down the corridor. I am not a psychic person, but a peculiar anticipation, a hint of dread, sometimes comes over me. It has the odd result of sharpening my powers of observation. I notice, and even hear, things which do not seem to impinge on me in the ordinary way. Now, as I hesitated with my hand on the doorknob, I began automatically to notice the smallest details near me: the radiator pipes, for example, and the place where the paint had been chipped off the end section—the difference in the colour of the chipped edges—and the slight mildew on an old notice that hung, a degree or two on the slant, by the door; and the fact that in the word NOTICE a serif had not printed on the E.

I opened the door, walked across the secretary's anteroom to the door on the other side, opened that, and went in.

Sir George Cayley was standing in the archway of the small annex that housed the bed and other modest furniture which the Deputy Commissioner kept for the nights he worked too late to go home. George Cayley was a small, plump, and immaculately dressed figure with a face like a Donatello cherub. He had turned his head when he heard the door open, and I was as surprised at the pain in his expression as I had been at the tone of his voice. He beckoned me with his head, and I went to stand beside him and look down at the woman who lay there on the camp bed.

Even at that moment, and seeing her in the distraught and awkward posture of misery, I experienced an impact of spirit and a certain tautness of the nerves. Perhaps half a dozen times in one's life one meets a person of outstanding calibre —I can only call it that—and whenever it occurs, and whatever the circumstances, the antennæ of one's mind are set violently quivering. Another reaction, in me, is that my usual composure and confidence is suffused with a curious blend of excitement and humility.

My old professor of medicine at Harvard * would, I am sure, have described this woman simply as "a superior person," and he was no snob. George Cayley told me afterwards that many people experienced the same "impact" on meeting her, and none seemed to revise their opinions unfavourably later. I had better say, however, that it was not a question of sex appeal, although she was handsome enough. Mercifully for me, I had never fallen in love with any of my patients.

She lay there on her back, breathing rapidly, and from time to time slowly opening her eyes, only to close them again with an expression of weary pain. She was a little over average height, perhaps, and aged somewhere in the thirties. By long habit a psychiatrist makes an automatic but

* There is no direct descendant of John Harvard, the founder. We are descended from a cousin, and only three of the family—two Englishmen and myself—have been to the university. I took my M.D. there and requalified in England.

careful scrutiny of his patients, and my eyes began their familiar routine. This woman was dressed in a grey coat and skirt, excellently cut, and I particularly noticed her shoes, which I thought must be American. Her white blouse had one simple golden clip at the throat—a clip made in the form of the Egyptian *ankh*. (I wondered if she knew its meaning, and made a mental note to ask her one day.) Her hands, one hanging down limp and white with slightly curled fingers, were well kept and were devoid of rings; the nail polish was only slightly tinted. The brown hair, now ruffled and twisted, had many—far too many—strands of grey for her age.

And then there was the face. It was a lovely but curious face, I thought—curious in its make-up of features which seemed to be at odds with one another. It was a severe face, with its wide brow and strong chin. But the great eyes, soft and green-gold, dominated it—even in its present distress— and seemed to communicate a simplicity and sweetness to the whole face.

I touched George Cayley on the arm and motioned him back into the main office.

"What has she been given so far?" I asked.

"Three Veganin and a lot of brandy," he answered. "What is the next thing to be done, Paul? I'll tell you all I know about the business later."

"Has she had an accident so far as you know, or is it something mental?"

"She didn't mention anything physical—no, I'm sure it's not that, from what she said."

"Good. I'll give her a quick examination just in case, and the best thing at the moment would probably be a long night's rest with plenty of dope. The question is, where can she go? I imagine you don't want her to go home, wherever 'home' is, and I would prefer her not to wake up in any place that spells hospital or nursing home." I paused; then what seemed a possible solution came to me. "What about Anne? I wonder if she could put her up and stay with her until she comes round?"

"Yes, I think that's a good idea. I'll get her here straight away while you look at Caroline."

"Caroline what?"

"Caroline Norton."

As I was removing things from my bag he was saying on the telephone, "I want you to find Anne Milbanke, Dr. Harvard's secretary—one of the three usual numbers will pick her up—and get her to come to me at Scotland Yard just as soon as she can." Then he sat quite still in the Deputy Commissioner's chair, staring at the wall opposite, his mind probably a long way off. I wondered what jobs Caroline Norton had done at the bidding of this composed and secret man, and which of these jobs he was now thinking of. The word "Intelligence" covered such a wide range of activity.

I returned to the little annex. There was nothing organically wrong with Caroline—I am generally going to call her that from now onwards—but she was in a very bad state. She had had some kind of severe mental shock and now, with the drink and drugs, she was lulled into a painful semiconsciousness and was only just aware of my presence. I sat back on the little hard chair in the room and looked at her for some moments. The familiar question formed itself. What was locked up in the myriad cells within that fine head? What was wreaking such havoc with an otherwise healthy human being? As I watched in silence, as so many psychiatrists had

7

watched their new patients, it was as if a multitude of invisible—but vitally real—electric wires spread out from the woman in front of me; wires which bound her to people and things and memories, and to the men and women of æons ago who had produced her. Some of these wires, stretching out who knows where, had now been put out of order; they had been cut, or crossed, or asked to bear the strain of currents they could not stand. And the result of this mysterious interference was that a woman was struggling in agony with an assailant that neither of us could see.

I got up and went back to George Cayley.

"Before Anne comes, give me an outline of how she got in this state."

"She rang me in Whitehall. I hadn't heard from her for some time. She is, as they say in the theatre, resting. We thought of retiring her, as she did not seem to have recovered enough to be absolutely her old self. But, unfortunately, there has recently arisen a state of affairs which may make her a key figure again. I can't tell you the details, but we have suddenly become aware of a small but very dangerous set-up in Europe and—such is the curious fortune of these things—the man we believe to be the mainspring of the group served with Caroline in the Resistance and was an intense admirer of hers. She has already seen him again, when she went over for a Resistance reunion. This new development may mean we have a chance in a million to get some information. He never, of course, knew of her connection with the Service. However, that is not the point at the moment. She has been living in the country with her parents, whom I have known for years, and they naturally have no idea of what she was doing, or might be doing, or that I was in any way connected with her work.

"After she was sent to rest," he continued, "I allowed her to see me for the first time, as the war was over and we did not intend to use her in peacetime for very dangerous missions. In view of what has now arisen I am beginning to regret my revelation. However, she was—as you can imagine— surprised to see an old family friend in the role of her chief, and immediately realized that I was responsible for getting her into our particular branch of Intelligence in the first place. We have been very good friends ever since, and she treats me much more like a father than she does her own father; and to me she is rather like a daughter, to which is added, on my side, an admiration that goes unusually deep. You can imagine what a relief it was when I no longer had to give, or hand on, orders that might mean her death on almost any day of the week; and what I feel now that I might have to do it again.

"Well, as I say, she rang me at my office, and I thought it was a friendly call. But she said quite simply and almost inaudibly, 'George, I'm ill—very ill. Can you possibly see me at once—anywhere you say—I can just make it.' That was an hour ago. I told her to get in a taxi and come straight here. I warned them downstairs, and one of the police matrons looked after her until I arrived. She was sitting hunched up in a chair, shivering. Her face was as white, drawn, and terrified as if she had been in the presence of the devil. All she said, and said very quietly, was, 'Oh, George, I don't think I can stand this much longer. I think I'm going mad. Just stay with me for a bit, will you, and try and get someone who can

9

dope me or do something.' The matron had just given her the Veganin, and I sent for some brandy. Then we half carried her up here when the Deputy Commissioner left; after that I phoned you and sat by her until she became drowsy. That's all I know."

He lit a cigarette and waited for a while, then went on. "Paul, I hope you will put her right—whatever it means, however long it takes. There is primarily the official reason, which makes it imperative that she get well enough for this job if we need her for it. Then, naturally, there are our personal reasons in the Service. It's strange; many of them never came back at all. Some have come back broken in mind, as you know. Of all those men and women, so many were just names, although some were naturally more real to us if we had to work closely with them. But there has always been something about Caroline Norton, some quality almost of nobility, that singled her out. On many occasions we had to order her to do things that seemed to spell certain destruction for her. In all the years I have been at this business I have never given such reluctant orders; and the others felt just the same about her. But there could be no favouritism, and that was that. Finally she came back to us, literally out of the jaws of the whale, and I have seldom seen tough people like some of my colleagues behave as they did. She for her part did not, and never will, know quite how much I was involved. I saw her fairly often without her knowing, but she was only allowed to see me—as I told you—after the war was over. Otherwise she could have described me, and the others, if she were captured and tortured—as she finally was. Caroline Norton certainly deserves well of her country.

"Tonight," he went on, "I shall have to give you as much

of the background as I possibly can. I may have to omit some facts, as they bear directly on the Service, but you are used to these evasions of ours, and if you really come against something in her case that needs more clarifying, I shall do my best to explain."

"You feel all this is connected with the Service, then?"

"That, Paul, is for you to tell me later on; but I have a feeling it must be. By the way, you will presumably want to see Caroline safely off to sleep, so we had better meet afterwards and have something to eat. For some reason I feel I want to get out of town; so, if you don't mind, let us have Martin drive us to a hotel I know of on the Thames near Maidenhead."

I had just said I thought it a good idea when Anne Milbanke came into the room and said good evening to us. With her graceful efficiency, her good looks, and her good clothes, she always seemed to bring a situation down to earth, acting as a catalyst on the emotions surrounding her. She had probably been out with a boy friend, and now her evening was completely ruined; but we would never know it. We exploited her ruthlessly, and she accepted it all as necessary or inevitable. George Cayley had sent her to me in 1939, and she still seemed to like the job. I remembered his remarks at the time: "You can't rattle that young woman, or surprise her, or upset her." And he had been right—mercifully, for all our sakes.

"Anne," I said, "I'm sorry if we've spoiled your evening. Can you put up a girl in your flat and stay with her until she is awake and capable of being brought to Wimpole Street tomorrow?"

"Of course, Paul," she answered. "Who and where is she?"

"Her name is Caroline Norton, one of Sir George's casualties—a very special one, by the way—and she is in there, in the night annex. She's had a very severe psychological shock —we don't yet know of what kind—and she must have a good sleep if we are to have any success tomorrow. I will come back with you and give her some fairly strong dope, and I want you to sit with her until she is definitely asleep. Then be in the room from about eight tomorrow until she wakes. She may take some time to come round; just bear with her and be very gentle. Get her dressed and phone me. Then bring her to Wimpole Street in a taxi. Don't forget to tell her you are a friend of Sir George's as soon as she can take in anything, and that you are taking her to see him straight away." I turned to George Cayley.

"Does Caroline know your handwriting well?" He nodded. "Then would you write her a note to reassure her. Anne can give it to her when she is awake."

So we supported Caroline Norton out of the office of the Deputy Commissioner, down the newly painted green corridor, into the lift, along the echoing ground floor, past the puzzled Sergeant Holmes, down the great stairway, and finally into the car. As I got in, George Cayley stood looking at Caroline as she sank back onto the cushions. "Look after her, Paul; I will pick you up at Anne's in about half an hour's time. Good-bye."

After dinner that night we sat in deck chairs on the grass embankment above the Thames, watching the dark flow of the water and looking across at the bulks of big trees faintly outlined against the sky. It was a very warm May evening, and the scene was peaceful and almost sentimentally picturesque. As we smoked in silence I went back in mind over the years I had worked with—I should really say "worked for"—this curious and most admirable man.

In the winter of 1938 I had been dining with a friend at the Athenæum and had, as if by chance, been introduced to a Sir George Cayley. I liked him at first sight but was too preoccupied at the time to dwell on him. I cannot even remember what we talked about. But a month or two afterwards my secretary told me she had made an appointment for a new patient—it was George Cayley—who had been recommended by our friend who had introduced us. I naturally thought that our previous meeting had been for the purpose of looking me over—a preliminary unofficial survey, which I would always recommend to anyone before going to an unknown psychiatrist for treatment, apart, of course, from looking him up in the medical directory.

However, the boot was to be placed rather firmly on the other foot. He had certainly contrived to look me over at the Athenæum, but for very different reasons.

He came quite quickly to the point, after he had made himself comfortable in my consulting room.

"Dr. Harvard," he said, "I am afraid this visit is a subterfuge. I have come to ask if you would consider working for certain sections of British Intelligence. We have, as you would imagine, made careful inquiries about you, and your main job would be to examine and assess certain men and women whom we want for our work—work mostly overseas—and other individuals who come into our hands and who are not particularly friendly. We should also want you to do other work from time to time, but the psychological investigations would be the most important. I am afraid it would

13

mean a complete disruption of your practice—except to keep some of it going as a good cover. It would mean virtually full-time work for us, and a considerable change in such things as your house, servants, and general routine."

"What makes you think I would be suitable or willing to do the job?" I asked rather stupidly, as I was genuinely surprised at this gambit, and was stalling for time.

"Well, it is a long story. You will understand me sympathetically if I tell you that you have been under investigation for a long time—solely, of course, with a view to our employing you. The first thing that particularly interested us was a talk with the Commissioner of Police, who said that his people sometimes called you in on matters of criminal psychology—in which field he said there were few, if any, better than yourself. That fitted very well with part of our plans, and an examination of your published papers—and other inquiries—showed you might well prove valuable in the non-criminal, but at the same time curious, psychology of what we may call 'agents.' Their mentalities are often a kind of counter-change pattern of the criminal, and some of the best of them are very peculiar characters.

"Then there were all sorts of other factors which made you a good 'possible' for our work. You are, for one thing, particularly devoted to this country in spite of—or perhaps because of—your American mother and American training. You are also a wealthy man—although, by the way, you will not find us niggardly about finance. Then there is your range of interests, from flying airplanes to the pursuit of the Old Masters."

He stopped, presumably to gauge the effect on me, and to see if I answered. I didn't; and I remember being amused

14

to note that anyone who talked of the "pursuit of the Old Masters" could not know or care much about paintings and the general history of art. Indeed, I found later it was one of his few blind spots. He was as indifferent to art as I am to good—I mean very good—music. But as he spoke I became more and more interested in his proposals, and I think unconsciously my mind had been made up from the first—probably on the irrational attraction I felt growing in me for this plump person from another world. For it proved indeed a world of shadows and fantasy-reality.

He continued to talk of my character, personality, interests, and habits—which, if it had done nothing else, would have given me a profound respect for whatever service carried on such investigations without its activities even being suspected for a moment.

Before he left I told him I was definitely interested in his offer but I must think it over, and all it implied for my career and my own pattern of personality. I said that my professional work was in any case drifting more and more towards diagnosis and research, and away from treatment, although I could get absorbed enough in the latter when I was doing it. I added that this new work, from what I gathered, would probably provide a profound professional interest.

On the subject of my house in Hampstead he was firm. It was much too isolated and rather too distant from Whitehall. I would have to move out and be installed in a large flat over the Porchester, where I would be both available and more anonymous.

Cayley told me he would have a detailed security investigation of Alfred and Sarah—who, by the way, were married—and that he had already planned for them to stay with me if at all possible. I think he realized how fond we were of one another; and, in the interests of all concerned, he was anxious to get them cleared. Alfred, who had been a sergeant in the Grenadier Guards—and who could be as close as a clam—seemed already to be potentially acceptable. As my chauffeur, he would obviously have to do and see things rather out of the ordinary.

Luckily both Alfred and Sarah were finally passed, and Alfred became an invaluable cog in the machinery that soon caught us up.

Fortunately my secretary was already engaged to a young doctor and was soon leaving to be married. Anne Milbanke was sent by Cayley to take her place, and she was a treasure indeed. Cayley always said that to be as "feather-bedded" as I was, especially after the arrival of Anne, was exceedingly bad for my character but suited his purpose well enough. He remarked that I was more useful to him if I did not have to worry about my material and human background; and I am afraid I agree with him.

Before I finally accepted this revolution in my affairs I asked George Cayley if he minded my checking with the Commissioner of Police as to his authority and status. He smiled but readily agreed, and said that the Commissioner knew in outline what had been proposed to me; also that there was every reason why I should go on with my police work, whenever it came my way. It too was excellent cover; and in any case he, Cayley, had a room in the Home Office building and was often in and out of Scotland Yard.

I went to see the Commissioner next day, and he said he had a vague idea of what I was in for, and of course had had to authorize a good many of the searching inquiries that had been made into my life and doings. He too smiled when I asked about George Cayley's authority and status.

"His authority is good enough," he replied. "The Prime Minister sent for me to tell me as much, on my own account, some years ago. But as for his status, no one knows; or rather I imagine only a handful of people do. But you and I will never know; and what's more I have no idea—and don't want to have—what outfit he belongs to, or runs. He and his kind have endless ramifications, both service and civilian. We touch him, of course, with our Special Branch, but they are mostly tied in with M.I.5, who have the perfectly clear job of coping with the internal security of the country—despite the newspapers' belief that they deal with everything from catching spies to sending Mata Haris to seduce tipsy generals."

He leaned back and pulled a copy of *Who's Who* out of a shelf. "Cayley's entry is a model of brevity and uninformativeness."

I had already looked him up in my own copy. The entry was certainly short. It read:

CAYLEY, Sir George, Kt., cr. 1930; M.C. 1917; b. 8 July, 1891; s. of late Richard Hugh Cayley, K.C. *Educ:* Wellington; Royal Military Academy, Woolwich. *Publication:* Mountaineering in the Jura, 1925. *Address:* Harley Manor, Frome, Somerset. *Clubs:* Athenæum, Brooks's.

And so I went to work for George Cayley, and I have never regretted it. Although I have met a number of men who were obviously senior in the Service—and very many other men and women up and down the scale—I am almost as ignorant today of the set-up and organization of the work as I was when I entered it. I have made a rough estimate of Intelligence functions and, idly, a number of more specific guesses from time to time; but few people, except those at the very hub of the business, are allowed to know much—and quite rightly. Therefore I shall refer to the organization as the "Service," which is quite sufficient. One learned of strange incidents, incredible bravery, and some unpleasant occurrences; and I myself have been involved in a number of cases, few of which I enjoyed, and out of which I was sometimes lucky to escape with a whole skin.

Now, as George Cayley started to talk, I heard what little background there was to be told of Caroline Norton.

"Her father is an ex-diplomat," he said, "and was in Switzerland for many years before the recent war. Caroline therefore spent a lot of her time there too. She always had two pronounced talents in addition to an unusual character. First, she was a born linguist and came to speak perfect German—proper German, as well as that strange flat kind they talk in Switzerland; her French is also good. Second, she developed an almost uncanny interest in wireless. She first learned odds and ends from her two brothers when she was little more than a toddler, and later on she took a course at Zürich University. She was always quite puzzled by her ability in this subject, because otherwise she had a normal girl's interests—such things as pictures, books, dress, and so on, and, of course, riding."

A sudden breeze rustled the trees around us for a minute or two and then subsided, and a rotund little motor cruiser helped to break our train of thought with its chugging sound as it swam downstream.

"What about her intellectual and religious interests, if any?"

"It's strange that you ask that. She has always been religious. Yet it was never quite the conventional Church of England faith of her parents, which rather worried the good souls. But she always pleased them by attending the little village church where they live. But when in England she often used to go off on her own, and it was once quite by accident that her parents discovered that she was helping with an East End mission and had worked herself nearly dead in the process.

"Then, some years before the war, I suggested to our people that she might be approached. I had known her and her family for years, and appreciated the background. Without her knowing anything about me, as I told you, she finally joined the Service and was sent to live in Germany, with all the necessary relations, pedigree, and previous history arranged for, of course. Incidentally, we changed her appearance to a remarkable degree by the quite simple expedient of having her pluck most of her eyebrows and wear her hair as short as possible. You would not believe what a curious change those two things made in her appearance."

"What about her emotional life?" I interrupted at that point. I wanted a little of the more human data before he went on with the story.

"Well, that has always puzzled me; but of course the work she did for us benefited greatly by what I can only describe as a certain indifference to the male approach. Perhaps I ought to go further: our reports on her—and these are supported by all sorts of small things I myself have observed and heard about her within the family circle—seem to show that she positively dislikes any emotional demonstration. I imagine you would substitute 'fears' for my word 'dislikes'—yes, 'fears' it must be, deep down. She seems to have many men friends, but if any of them show signs of stepping over some invisible line, they are, shall we say, dismissed. There is, however, one very decent fellow, a man who lives near her family's place and who had a remarkable war record—he is out of the Army now—who seems to be devoted to her but is wise enough not to be demonstrative. She seems to like him a lot, or so her parents say. I have never met him and I can't remember his name.

"As I said, this emotional self-containment, which is accompanied by a delightful talent for ordinary human relationships, made her an excellent worker in the Service." George Cayley paused and then added, "One odd thing about Caroline, when taken with what I have just said, is her eye for good clothes. I think it is her elegance—and you should see her in a full evening turnout—that so confuses the would-be suitors. And they have included some very fine types, I can assure you. I am thoroughly sorry for them."

Another pause, and he leaned back his head and blew a column of cigarette smoke straight up into the still night air. One always knew that this volcanic gesture meant that George Cayley had come to the end of a period; he had completed what he felt was one definite stage in the story.

What he had said about Caroline seemed to be forming a slight but definite pattern in my mind. She was beginning to live in my imagination.

"Now about her job; how much can you tell me of what happened to her; and, most important, have any actual incidents come back to you? Memorable incidents in which Caroline took part and which might involve strain or pain or exceptional perplexity? You mentioned torture at Scotland Yard. What was that about?"

"Well, I can tell you this much. She did some perilous jobs inside Germany, mostly as a reporter of radio installations and related activities, but she always survived them. Then it finally got too hot for her, and we pulled her back discreetly into Switzerland for a rest, before sending her to work with the French Resistance as an expert in radio sabotage. So far as our reports go, she was bearing the work remarkably well, and we only took her out of Germany when we heard that they were on to her. She loves Switzerland, and the rest there did her a lot of good; incidentally, we followed the line you advised at that time. One of our people questioned her about any experience she might have had which would have been a particular strain, and asked if she had had any specific shock she could recall. She said she was under considerable tension quite often, that she was used to it, but that otherwise nothing definite in the form of a painful event weighed on her at all. So we put her with the Maquis, and just before the Germans collapsed her unit was betrayed. There was time, however, for them to question her, and they don't seem to have got anything out of her at the beginning. Then they tortured her and did get a story out of her before she collapsed and nearly died. We know all this because we captured the Abwehr and Gestapo papers of that particular interrogation centre, and the whole of her case was carefully documented."

"And did she betray anyone or anything before she collapsed?" I asked. I had a very clear picture of that young

21

woman and the contempt she would probably show her jailers.

"She put up an extraordinary fight over some weeks, but inevitably the time came when she could not stand it any longer and broke. But even the Germans put on record their grudging admiration of her behaviour."

Quite a tone of triumph seemed to dominate George Cayley's words, which I could not understand.

"You see," he went on, "the story she told them was a brilliant fake—halting, plausible, and impossible to check on, except after weeks of investigation. They would, of course, have found her out in the end; but the concentration camp she was sent to was overrun by the Americans before they could do much. She had collapsed completely after her 'confession' and was very ill until she was rescued."

"And after that?"

"Oh, we brought her back—or rather we sent her to her beloved Switzerland for a long convalescence first. By the way, she had lost much of the memory of her questioning, including the actual torture. As I told you, we wanted to keep her ready for a new job; but I have let her do much as she pleased for a considerable time. I see her from time to time, and she always seems calm and happy in a rather reserved kind of way. She has lived quietly with her parents and spends her time reading and riding, with frequent visits to London for the art galleries and for concerts. Paintings, music, and horses seem to be her chief pleasures. However, she has seemed tired and a little distrait at times, and she does not seem to have enough energy to do any regular job, even if we wanted her for one. It always seems to me as if she were recharging her batteries, to use a favourite phrase of yours. Her parents don't know a thing about her work, of course, and believe she was in a secret WAAF job in the war, which she could not get away from. It has always puzzled them why she wrote so seldom, and they were rather hurt about that. One day I shall have to tell them something, and I think the story will be a half-truth. I shall say that she spent the whole time since the fall of France working with the Maquis. You see, she was given an M.B.E.—just as a token—for unspecified 'Special Services.' She never mentions it herself, but it made her parents happy, and they would be happier still if they thought she had been in action, so to speak. And it was given, by the way, for her work with the Maquis—members of the Service don't get gongs for their work as such, except some of the stuffed shirts like me. I forgot to say that I rung the Nortons before I met you and told them Caroline had had to come to town to clear up some urgent problems related to her old Air Ministry job—a lame explanation, but good enough, which she herself will confirm by letter."

I was glad to get back to my flat that night. The whole of the Caroline case had kept me and my imagination—and my admiration—at full stretch for some hours. As I was taken up in the lift, away from the busy foyer of the Porchester, I felt as if I were being airborne to the clouds. It was escape that I needed just at that moment, escape to my possessions and the peace of my rooms, and especially the peace of contemplating my pictures. My batteries, too, need frequent recharging. After Sarah had brought me a whisky and hot water, I sat for a full quarter of an hour in front of a small Italian panel painting. I had bought it during the war, the day after I had failed to save one of George Cayley's agents—a man who had poisoned himself in his Whitehall flat. The little picture was by an unknown fifteenth-century Umbrian; it showed the Resurrection of Christ taking place in an exquisite mountainous landscape, floating in blue air, with tall feathery trees standing quietly on either side of the tomb.

I arrived at my Wimpole Street consulting room next morning at a few minutes before ten. Anne had telephoned twice to the flat to report that our patient had not yet woken up. So I set about clearing away a number of unimportant appointments for the next few days, but retaining for the moment my hospital afternoon (which George Cayley had agreed to my keeping when at all possible) and two private patients who were in a rather dependent stage. I then rang up the airfield at White Waltham and put off my week-end lesson on a new type of helicopter that the Sikorsky Company had turned out. (Since I took my private pilot's licence, the advent of the helicopter has appealed to me most; but one had to take a separate "ticket" for each type.) After that I sank into my patients' armchair and began to reread Flügel's *Psychology of Clothes* until the telephone rang and Anne said she would be along with Caroline in about half an hour. She reported her as "sort of numb and very pale." I telephoned George Cayley, and he said he would come over at once.

We sat there in my room, smoking, saying little, and—for my part—with a sense of expectancy coupled with a certain amount of misgiving. When Caroline finally came in she again cast her spell over me. But at least she was, so to say, moving under her own volition and in quiet, although obviously troubled, possession of herself. As Anne had said, she indeed looked pale, but her beauty was striking. She went straight over to Cayley and took his outstretched hand in both of hers—an easy spontaneous gesture of trust which was accompanied only by the quietly spoken words, "Thank you, George, very much, for looking after me last night." And before he could answer she turned to me and said with a trace of a sad smile, "You are Dr. Harvard—Anne said you had looked after me last night. I hope I was not too much trouble." She had a way, a rather charming way, of slightly inclining and then raising her head as she spoke.

From her bearing, her manner, and her careful choice of words, I knew then and there that Caroline Norton was not going to help me much with her treatment. I was sure that if I could do anything for her it would be only through indirect means, or perhaps by mechanical or chemical means. I had the distinct impression that she would resent any deep probing into her mind and would disapprove of anyone who attempted it. I felt the misgiving deepen into depression, a state made more irksome by my spontaneous regard and admiration for her. She must have sensed something of what was going on in my mind as she sat on one of my straight-backed chairs—the deep easy chair, I felt sure, would represent to her something feeble and helpless, and therefore to be resisted—and turned to George Cayley.

"I expect you have told Dr. Harvard about me, George. I am terribly sorry to have broken down like this, and I hope he will be able to do something to steady me. I will do my best to cooperate with him. Can I talk about the work if necessary?"

"Yes, Caroline, you can tell him anything that's necessary,

but avoid description of actual methods if you can, although he probably knows most of them. He has done our courses, and we have worked together for years; and"—this was said almost apologetically—"you can trust him completely."

And so it was that Caroline became my patient—the most lovely, enraging, and uncooperative patient any psychiatrist could have. She knew, of course, that there was something wrong with her, but thought of it as her own weakness, which, if I perhaps gave her a clue or even a drug, she could put right on her own and then be able to turn her back forever on the distasteful business of psychiatry. Like so many people, she did not believe in magic, but demanded it all the same. Needless to say, I never cured Caroline. Events cured her. All I can claim—and indeed must claim, for my conceit—is that I precipitated those events, interpreted some of them correctly, and used them for her benefit.

The first symptom of trouble, so far as she could tell me, had occurred suddenly only a few nights before I saw her at Scotland Yard. She had been listening to a broadcast account of a woman who had worked with the French Resistance, and that night she had a bad nightmare. Next morning, to her surprise and annoyance, she found herself frightened of going out alone. Thinking this to be sheer foolishness, she fought the feeling and went down to the village, but soon came back feeling more frightened than ever, and shaking all over.

From then onwards she was too frightened to venture out at all. She was afraid to go to sleep, and when she did drop off through sheer weariness she had severe nightmares and woke up again, sweating profusely. After a few days and nights of this agony, which was complicated by her having to deceive her parents, she decided—terrified as she was—to come to London and ask George Cayley for advice, hoping at the same time that the change of scene might help her to break out of the vicious circle she felt contracting about her.

I asked her about the nightmares.

"They were always the same. A woman, or rather the shadow, almost, of a woman, would slowly approach, and it would put out its hand as if to touch me. Then I would want to scream and would wake up shivering with fright."

"And the woman?" I asked. "Could you never see her face or get any idea of who—or what—she was?"

"No, Dr. Harvard, the face was always a blur. I have no idea who she is. All I can think of is she may be someone connected with my Service work in Germany or France."

I asked her to go over the broadcast very carefully, as it was obvious that it had started this time-bomb ticking in her mind. But she could tell me nothing except that it was exciting and accurate, and that her own experiences had been similar. The *Radio Times* announcement did not help us and did not jog her memory. We talked over her life in general during an interview or two, but she was reserved to a marked degree about anything emotional, although she did her best to think back to her Service days and their human problems in order to help me.

She had gone back with Anne to the flat, after our second interview—she couldn't bear to be left alone, even for an instant—when I thought of something. I rang up a friend of mine in the B.B.C.

"Henry," I said, "can you do something for me? I am particularly interested in a broadcast I heard about last week; it touches on a rather important problem I have on hand. If it was recorded, could you get it run through for us in one of your listening rooms?"

He took down the title of the feature and said he would do his best. He rang back a quarter of an hour later to say I was lucky—it had been recorded—and to fix a time for us to hear it that evening.

At ten minutes past nine the three of us, Caroline, Anne, and myself, sat in a small grey room in the basement of Broadcasting House. The broadcast was of a familiar type— the story dramatized, with actors speaking the dialogue, and another voice giving the narrative and connecting pieces. It was well produced and came over with conviction.

Caroline was listening with great concentration, and I knew she was making a genuine effort to find a clue to her feelings. But her expression remained unchanged until about halfway through the programme. At that point the heroine was captured by the Germans, rather as Caroline herself had been, and was taken to an interrogation centre. She was still "acting innocent" there, as the Germans had only pulled her in on suspicion. She was taken into a room, and we heard the German guard say, "Sit down here and vait." Then there was the sound of a door opening, and a woman's voice with a strong German accent and an oily and ingratiating tone said, "And now, Mademoiselle, perhaps you vill answer some zimple questions."

At these words Caroline became as rigid as if she were in a cataleptic trance. Then she said, "It's that voice; it's her," and she went limp, breathing hard and passing her hand across her eyes. The radio voice started another sentence and then was faded out, to be followed by a German man's voice.

Caroline seemed to recover after a minute or two and

29

turned to me. "Can we turn it off, Dr. Harvard?" she asked rather briskly. I turned off the set and went back to my seat.

"It was that voice that started your nightmare?"

She sat silent for a moment, then: "Yes, I suppose it must have been, although I can't imagine who it reminds me of. It must be someone in the interrogation centre I was taken to. I can't remember a lot about that, so—yes, it *must* be connected with that time."

We had arranged that Anne should take her for a country drive next day, and Alfred motored them down to the Sussex coast. Caroline seemed a little calmer, so Anne said, and next day I decided to tell her what I wanted to do.

In some of these violent repressions a rather violent cure can be effected by putting the patient under one of a variety of drugs or gases, and getting him to live through the experience that is suspected of harbouring the danger. I was sure that we could get something out of her by this abreaction method, but I was not at all certain that she would agree to the treatment. The fact that she might not remember all she said would make her wary of committing herself to the experiment. I was always to be aware of this battle between Caroline and myself. She resented most deeply and genuinely the fact that anyone should have an opportunity of invading her mental privacy. It is a common and quite reasonable point of view; but when the health of a patient can depend upon his or her utter frankness, it is a source of considerable exasperation if he resists your efforts to help him. I once explained to Caroline that my inquiries about her emotional life were for her own especial benefit, and that sex—if sex arose—was as dreary a topic to a psychiatrist as manure is to the gardener, but just as important. She bent her head a little and said very gently, "Dr. Harvard, you know there are certain things I would rather not discuss, and it would be so much easier if we avoided them."

I told Caroline I would like her to have an ether abreaction, and explained what it would mean. I did not fail to point out that it would stir her up mightily, but that it might well mean a major step towards making her better. I added that it was extremely unlikely that she would reveal anything, except about her fears—and that, even if she did, it would be unimportant to all concerned. I even offered to have everything she said taken down on a tape recorder so that she could hear it played back afterwards. But she refused. Nor did she give any reasons, or say what it was she was afraid of revealing. She knew, of course, that I knew it must be one of a fairly well-mapped series of fears or anxieties. But she could not find it in herself to trust me. She was not at the moment in a bad enough state to have to. However, that was not to last long.

Soon after her refusal she arrived for a session, and she was in a very bad state—almost as bad as when I had first seen her. Anne had to help her onto my couch—the first and last time she occupied it—and I regarded her with new concern, wondering what added complication had now arisen. It was, I found, only a quarter of an hour back that the blow had fallen, when they were coming to see me. They were on top of a Number 25 bus, and it had become wedged in the traffic halfway up Bond Street. They were talking, and Caroline had casually glanced down at the crowded pavement. Suddenly she had grasped Anne's arm like a vice. Anne had half-risen and looked down too, trying to see who or what it was that had caused such a violent reaction in her compan-

31

ion. The person she picked out, and who she was sure was the target of Caroline's eyes, was walking in the opposite direction to the bus; all that could then be seen was the back view of a tall robust woman in smart tailor-mades—"I particularly remember her rather bold bottom," Anne briskly told me later, annoyed that she could remember little else. The bus had then started to move, and the figure was hidden from view. That woman, said Caroline, had been the woman of her dream; the face had been visible only for an instant, but it was certainly the face which the dream had lacked.

"I felt paralysed at the sight of her; yet I had to go on looking as she walked away. But the back of her told me nothing, and I have still no idea who it was; but at least I am sure now that I fear a real woman and that I saw her today. I don't know what is happening to me, Dr. Harvard." At that she started to cry, silently at first, and then with long despairing sobs. As she brought her hands to her face she turned over on her side.

I pressed the bell on my desk as I rose, and went on tiptoe to the door. Anne appeared. I glanced towards the couch and went out. I opened the front door, stepped out of the house, and pulled my cigarette case from my pocket. Wimpole Street was basking quietly in the spring sunshine. A pompous woman, overdressed to absurdity, went by, towing behind her a reluctant Pekinese. As I drew in the smoke I half-closed my eyes and saw in my mind the crowded pavement and the sudden flash of recognition in Caroline as she glanced down from the bus. I thought of how foreshortened people look at that angle, how a face from above can so

32

easily be mistaken. On balance, it was doubtful if that was *the* woman, although I did not quite know why I doubted it. It was just that I sensed the situation to be in some way unreal. If Caroline had had such a shock of recognition, it was probably some woman whose face resembled the memory. But, on the other hand, the woman may have been our enemy, walking confidently down Bond Street. That there was a real woman somewhere in the background I had no doubt. Yesterday evening I had asked George Cayley to have the records checked urgently to see if any woman had been involved in Caroline's interrogation and torture. He had not yet had any news.

"Paul, I think she is better now." It was Anne's voice over my shoulder. I turned and went in out of the sun.

"Anne, get on to the matron at Byron House and see if she can let me have a room and the necessary crew this evening for an ether abreaction. I must, of course, get Caroline to agree to have it. I don't believe she saw her devil today, but devil there must be—or must have been—and I am going to take a chance on the whole cauldron being made to boil up artificially. I'm going to ask her now, and I would like you to be there tonight, as she is so fond of you. She will probably need you afterwards."

When I returned to the consulting room Caroline was lying on her back on the sofa. I sat down at my desk and waited.

"I have never cried in front of a man before," she said, still looking up at the ceiling. "I'm sorry." Then, after a moment or two: "Why did you leave me, Dr. Harvard? I thought psychiatrists were used to weeping women—and even encouraged them." Feeling anger at herself for such a display of human weakness, she seemed now to be diverting some of it onto me.

"I left because you didn't want me in the room."

"Why should you have thought that?" she asked. I wished that other part of her would not go on fighting me, but she could not help it.

"It was really quite simple. You started crying, realized where you were, became ashamed of yourself—or so I thought—and turned over on your side, away from me. To cry in front of me was to lower yourself in your own eyes and to exhibit weakness before me. I think you feel it is in some way to put yourself in my power to exhibit weakness to me."

A slight flush mounted from her throat to her cheeks. I went on, "Caroline, don't you see that you can never be in my power and I don't want you in my power? Please try to understand that a psychiatrist's job is to bring about just the opposite—to get his patients into a position where they can never be in the power of anyone or anything. At present you are in the power of something in your own mind. All I want is for you to be released from it, whatever it is. But to achieve that you must help me; and the best help you can give is to sacrifice a little of your pride—just a little."

"I'm sorry, Dr. Harvard. What do you want me to do?" She spoke very quietly and slowly.

I then said that I thought it essential for her to go into the nursing home immediately and let me try the treatment on her.

She said almost inaudibly, "All right; if I must go through

with it, I must. What will you tell the nurses and people about me?" At last she was being human.

"I shall tell them part of the truth—that you have been ill ever since you were in the hands of the Gestapo."

Caroline lay asleep in the high nursing-home bed.

Anne still held her right hand as it lay white and still on the blanket. I was so exhausted that I sat slumped in the small armchair, looking first at one, then at the other of those two exceptional young women. But I was satisfied—for the moment. We had wrestled with the devil, and the devil had revealed himself, or rather herself, to us. As I had questioned Caroline under that evanescence of ether she had slipped back over the years into a whitewashed torture cell of the Gestapo.

To all of us the experience we had lived through an hour ago will, I am sure, remain vividly and terribly in our memories forever. There were the two nurses, and Anne and myself. As those forgotten days came back to Caroline she relived them in pain and terror. But, freed by the anæsthetic from the iron self-control with which she had faced the Germans, she had fought with the two nurses like a wild animal. She was really fighting a woman called Helga Bamberg; I at last knew the name of our enemy.

Next morning I was leaning out of my window, staring at the expanse of Hyde Park stretching away towards Kensington Palace; the rounded tops of the trees looked like great green clouds seen from above. Having reached one milestone in the Caroline case, I was suddenly possessed by the longing for mountains. I never climb mountains, but looking at them is one of the great pleasures of my life. The Rockies, the Tyrol, Switzerland, the Dolomites—they were all places where I could achieve that mixture of excitement and serenity which, along with certain paintings, provided the most effective restoration of my personality. I started idly planning my escape.

I had really been quite hard pressed for over a year, and even night work had become the rule rather than the exception. I felt I deserved a holiday, and the business of Caroline Norton was also proving a considerable strain, chiefly, I am afraid, because I had allowed my emotions to be too much involved.

As I was considering this aspect of the case the telephone rang. It was Cayley. He had had a transcript of Caroline's interrogation sent to him, and he blamed himself for not having remembered about a woman named Helga Bamberg. I told him I was glad of the corroboration, but merely confronting Caroline with the name would have elicited nothing. She had had to be made to bring the experience back into semiconsciousness and relive it. I also added that the effect on her of filling in this painful gap in her memory was unpredictable. Two or three interviews would be necessary to assess her attitude. If she came out in a calm state, it would probably be best to send her away for a holiday—preferably abroad—and make a complete break.

After three meetings at Wimpole Street, I found Caroline in a strangely mixed frame of mind. She was definitely calmer; she could now go out alone with only mild discomfort, and she was having better nights. Towards me she was more trusting but yet almost resentful—resentful in the

36

way a child might be towards a stranger who has unintentionally stumbled on a cherished secret. I was sure it was this old trouble about feeling she was in my power. But the central point of her case was still the enemy, Helga Bamberg, and here she exhibited a curious attitude. There was no doubt that she was greatly relieved at knowing who it was that had tormented her in reality and had since been tormenting her unconsciously. But despite the relief and her realization that she was reacting to the past, she was convinced that Helga Bamberg was alive and, in some way she could not grasp, was still a danger to her. It was as if one component of her unconscious fears had survived and was masquerading as a real fear that the woman was alive and threatening.

"In what way do you feel she is a danger?" I asked.

"I don't know," she answered. "I do all I can to face it and see what it is that I am afraid of; but I always come to the same conclusion—that she is alive and that I am afraid of her. I suppose you would call it a persecution complex or something."

And there it was, a much less soluble problem, insofar as fantasy and reality were now in league to bedevil her. So I decided to see what she felt about a holiday, a change of scene and enough time for her mind and feelings to reach a new and reposeful balance. Then we could perhaps get down to the problem with a new determination and a fresh approach. Caroline at once took to the idea, and when I offered Anne as a companion she was, in her quiet way, almost effusively grateful. She was not only glad to get rid of me—and out of my influence—but part of her, I am sure, was pleased at turning the tables on me by taking away my own secretary.

She chose Paris as her holiday base-camp. She had always been fond of the city and had never had opportunity enough to explore it as she had wished. Anne was also enthusiastic, and so the matter was settled.

Alfred motored us down to Dover on a glorious sunny morning, and the countryside, recently drenched with rain, scintillated and sparkled with light. I was so glad to see Caroline looking well that I could have sung. All I did was to smile rather aimlessly at everything along the road.

"That light sparkling on the fresh leaves reminds me," I remarked, "of the way Constable sometimes litters his landscapes with delicate little spots of bright pigment."

Caroline turned her head so sharply that I thought she had been hit by something. But her great green-gold eyes, as they met mine, held a peculiar expression. For the first time she looked at me with what I can only describe as approval, but there was amazement there too. I think I had suddenly graduated, with that one remark, from a tiresome but necessary encroachment on her life to an actual human being.

"Since when, Dr. Harvard, have you been interested in art?" she asked.

"Since I was at Harrow, at the age of fourteen, to be exact. But why are you so surprised?" I asked in my turn.

"I don't really know; but I never connected you with anything like that. You always seem so—"

"So analytical and materialistic was what you were going to say, wasn't it?" I laughed.

She blushed. "That wasn't fair; no, I just never thought of you as being interested in art."

"I can only answer in the words of Sir Thomas Browne,"

38

I said. " 'I can look a whole day with delight upon a handsome picture, though it be but of an horse.' "

I watched the boat as it stood away from the quay with bells sounding, ropes splashing into the water, and seagulls gracefully circling the masts. Caroline and Anne had just appeared on deck, and after I had waved my hat they caught sight of me and waved back. Then the vessel gathered speed and was soon away through the harbour mouth and headed for France.

I went back to the car, wondering, as I so often did, where the Caroline case would take me, and if I could ever really help to smooth her path. As I settled down into the seat, the seat Caroline had occupied, I felt my hip touch something which must have become lodged between the side of the car and the deep cushion. I moved over and fished out a small book. It was Evelyn Underhill's edition of *The Cloud of Unknowing,* that severe but beautiful treatise by a fourteenth-century English mystic whose identity continues still to elude the scholars. I leaned forward and pushed aside the glass panel behind Alfred's head.

"Alfred, did you happen to notice if Miss Norton was carrying any books when she got into the car in London?"

"Yes, Mr. Paul, as a matter of fact I did. She had a bundle of magazines and one or two books under her arm when she got in. Has she left them behind?"

"I think she dropped one of them, but we can easily send it on if she wants it."

I lay back in the sunlight and closed my eyes. A small door had opened for me, a door to part of Caroline's character. I began to see a little way into what had so puzzled me. And yet I realized, with a slight sinking of the heart, that although I had now taken another step towards her, it was a step that revealed more difficulties as well as more light.

For some minutes I debated whether to send the book on to her or not. I finally decided to keep it for the time being and say nothing.

$$3$$

With Caroline safely in Paris and apparently enjoying herself, I prepared to take a flying Wednesday-to-Wednesday holiday with some friends who had a fairy-tale villa on Lake
Garda. Most doctors have to go through intricate motions
before they take even a day or two off; and psychiatrists have
the added difficulty of dependent patients who may sometimes be in acute distress if they cannot see their doctors
at short notice. My special work made it even worse, as
George Cayley was a hard taskmaster. But after laying down
foolproof lines of communication for every minute of my
journey and the stay at Malcesine, I said good-bye to Sarah
and went down to the car, where Alfred's cheerful face
greeted me.

We drove to Northolt, and I climbed on board the ten-
o'clock plane for Milan. It was an excellent service, and we
were flying direct. We should land at Milan about three.
From there I should be met by car, and that evening the
Langleys and I would be sitting on the lakeside terrace of
the Villa Campagnola, sipping our cocktails, surrounded by
the most peacefully perfect scenery I know. As we crossed the
French coast I sent down a silent greeting to Caroline and
Anne, then lay back and dozed, thinking of George and Nellie Langley. They had built, to mix metaphors, an oasis there
by the lake, surrounded by their cypresses, cacti, palms, and

olives, and with my favourite oleanders in pink, yellow, or white; to say nothing of the seasonal flowers in beds and pots all round the house. I remember thinking about George's new book before I finally went off to sleep, hypnotized by those two roaring motors and the slightly stuffy cabin. I had asked the stewardess to wake me up when we flew in sight of the Alps, and after what seemed but a minute she shook me gently by the shoulder.

"The mountains, Dr. Harvard," she said in a low and amused voice, as if humouring a child; "but there's this for you too. It just came over the radio." She handed me a twist of paper from a radio book. "The captain is wondering what sort of a V.I.P. he has on board who can have personal radio messages sent during the flight!"

I looked at the message. It read: ASK PASSENGER DOCTOR HARVARD CONTACT BRITISH CONSUL REPRESENTATIVE MILAN AIRPORT ON LANDING URGENT BOSH. There was of course no signature, but George Cayley had added our code-word for the day, except that the eminent Flemish painter had had his name reduced en route to the familiar expletive of idiocy.

I looked up at the pretty girl; she now stood there eyeing me with that peculiar expression some people reserve for the great or the near-great. "Oh," I said, remembering what she had said about the captain, "I'm no one very special; but I am in the toils of a very demanding patient." This was evidently the right and modest thing to say, as she gave me a fresh smile. But what was troubling me was that my carefully planned little holiday was in ruins before it had even begun, and I felt quite certain that Caroline was the cause of it.

As we landed at Milan airport and came trundling round

42

the periphery track, I had become used to the idea of my broken leave, and pretended I was just on another job which involved flying to Italy and then flying back again, just for the fun of it. In the reception hall a tall lean man in a blue suit came up to me, identified himself as a servant of our consulate, and gave me a letter. It was from the consul, and said that Sir George Cayley wanted me to go straight away to Paris and see a Miss Norton; also that he wanted me to report to him as soon as possible to say what was wrong.

I thanked the man and asked him if by chance he knew how soon I could take off. He went one better—our Service efficiency was certainly up to scratch on details that day. There was an R.A.F. Dakota en route from Cairo and Rome, which was leaving for Paris in an hour. So I scribbled a note for Nellie and gave it to the chauffeur to take back, then sent a telegram to George Cayley and deliberately misspelled the word "Bosch." I sat down on the terrace to twiddle my mental thumbs and watch the airliners come and go. Finally an R.A.F. flight lieutenant came up and asked if I was Dr. Harvard. He said he was ready to go when I was. So off I went for the second time that day, but on this occasion in considerable discomfort; the aircraft was a freighter, and only the sketchiest seating had been rigged for three itinerant servicemen and myself. However, I asked the pilot to go as near the Alps as his flight course would allow without his getting into trouble, and we had a good view of the snow-covered peaks and Mont Blanc in the distance. On the whole I do not like mountains from the air, as they tend to get dwarfed and ironed out, but it was better than nothing.

I tried not to be irritated with George Cayley and Caroline, but did not succeed; so I thought of various ways I

43

could misspell our code-words for the week, which happened all to be artists' names beginning with B: Bosch, Botticelli, Blake, Boucher, Bermejo, Baldovinetti, Baldung, and Brueghel. I had got as far as Bottichelsea and Bake when I decided I was being childish and began doing some favourite observation exercises to while away the uncomfortable hours. I started by making mental notes of the ears of my companions and was delighted to see that one fellow, a very small flight sergeant, had the biggest tragus I have ever seen. I would have to draw that tragus for Chief Inspector Watkins at the Yard, who loved ears and himself looked exactly like Bertillon; indeed, he was probably the famous French detective reincarnated in the rival establishment.

At Bourget I found Anne waiting for me and looking very smart in a light brown frock. (Where was Caroline? I wondered, fearing she was in some hospital.) But her face was not as calm as usual, and there was a very marked tension in the way she moved.

"Oh, Paul, I'm so very sorry to break into the one little holiday you had planned. But I rang Sir George this morning, and he thought it best to get you. It's Caroline, of course; she's seen that woman again and is back in her terror, although thoroughly ashamed of herself, poor dear. She's here now."

"Here now!" I exclaimed. "What on earth for?"

"Well, it's really a kind of tribute to you, but she wouldn't admit it. At first she didn't want me to send for you; then, when Sir George said it was essential, she veered round and began counting the minutes until you arrived. When I told her you were coming by air, she insisted I bring her to meet you. With an unnecessary show of tact she remained over there—but within sight of me—so that I could speak to you alone first."

We walked into the passengers' lounge and went towards the wicker armchair that supported a very wan Caroline. She rose to greet me, and her eyes were sad and strained. But there was a difference between this Caroline, no matter how bad she felt, and the woman I had first seen at Scotland Yard. I think it was a substratum of anger and determination which was making itself felt. For that I was glad. If angry and determined, she would be a better ally in whatever was ahead.

She apologized very charmingly for ruining my holiday and seemed genuinely glad to see me. On the way out to the car, and all the way back to Paris, she forced herself to be cheerful, and we discussed her favourite pictures in the Louvre, and a variety of other subjects that drifted by. I knew she would start, in her own good time, to tell me what had happened. But it was not to be until the three of us were in the sitting room of their hotel suite. I had sent for drinks, but she would not touch them, so Anne and I drank ours alone and waited.

"I have seen her again, Dr. Harvard," began Caroline at last, "or rather not her herself, but a picture of her. And that means she is still alive, or how else could it have been painted? Because it is a new picture."

I asked her to describe in detail what she had done, seen, and felt; and this was her story.

She had been shopping with Anne that morning and, after buying some gloves, they had wandered aimlessly through the streets, stopping here and there, looking in shop windows and enjoying the crowds and the bustle and the sunlight. They came to the Pont des Arts, spent some minutes leaning over the side, and then crossed the river. A little later they found themselves in the rue Bonaparte (it was Anne who noticed the name in order to tell me) and were sauntering past one of those rather expensive-looking art shops that abound in Paris. Caroline said that they had almost passed the shop when her eye was caught by a picture prominently displayed on an easel in the window. She pulled Anne round, and they both stared at the thing, Caroline showing the same symptoms as when she had seen the woman on the pavement in Bond Street. There, she said, was a portrait of Helga Bamberg. It was not done as a portrait, but the face of Helga Bamberg was used for the face of the historical figure. It was a grim picture, Anne added. It showed the infamous Marquise de Brinvilliers, most famous of seventeenth-century poisoners, on her way to execution.

I brought their account to an end by getting up.

"You two stay here. I am going to see if I can get a look at that picture now. I am not going to take the chance of its being sold tomorrow, however slight that might be. Anne, did you happen to notice the name of the shop? It doesn't much matter, as I can easily walk the length of the street."

But she had remembered it. The shop was the Galerie Houdon. As it was growing dark, I went down to the porter's desk, took a torch out of the light luggage I had left there, walked out, and hailed a taxi.

The Galerie Houdon obviously catered to the moderately well-off foreigner who wished to purchase soapy academic nudes, classical subject pieces, and historical representations, all of them meticulously painted, and all highly satisfactory for those who needed such deplorable objects. And right in the middle of the window was the picture I had come to see. It was now quite dark, and there was only a ghostly shape on the easel; but I could see, from Anne's description, that it was the "Helga." Just as I was pulling out my torch a policeman strolled by and was mildly interested in the obvious Englishman who stood gazing into a dark window with a flashlight in his hand. So I said to him that I had only just found the shop a friend of mine had recommended, and the picture I sought was almost invisible.

"I hope you won't think I'm a potential burglar, *Monsieur l'Agent*, if I have a look at it with my torch," I said laughingly, playing the damn-fool foreigner.

"No, Monsieur, I do not think anything of the kind, but I think I will stay and keep you company, all the same."

So under the watchful gaze of a half-suspicious French *gardien de la paix* I had my first sight of Helga Bamberg, or at any rate what stood clearly and terrifyingly for Helga Bamberg in Caroline's mind. As Anne had said, the picture showed the Marquise de Brinvilliers. There is a well-known contemporary study by Le Brun of her on the way to the scaffold, and the present artist had obviously borrowed the idea from it. The original drawing in the Louvre shows only a fat, pathetic figure in a loose robe, as she sits huddled in the cart, clutching a small cross. The present artist had taken the motif and transformed it into a handsome but arrogant woman going defiantly to her death, with the driver of the cart looking lewdly over his shoulder at his attractive cargo. A curious omission was the cross. The face of this woman was indeed interesting, and I kept my torch for a long time trained on her features.

Quite a few people had by this time been attracted by the

strange spectacle of a man shining a torch through a shop window, with a policeman looking on.

"I think Monsieur would do well to finish his examination; he is collecting a crowd," the policeman said kindly but firmly. I had no intention of stopping, so with regret I resorted to pull.

"What I am doing is rather important, Monsieur. I am well known to Superintendent Claudel of the Police Judiciaire, and I assure you he would support me."

The name acted like the proverbial charm. "Ah, that is different," he said, "it is the crowd which must now move, not you." And he promptly ordered them off and became both my ally and my protector for the further, and somewhat lengthy, period of my examination.

That face in the picture was the face I would have imagined Messalina to have had—strong, handsome, arrogant, and cruel. And the figure too—what one could imagine of it beneath the robe—large and boldly proportioned, suggested what I had always felt Claudius's troublesome wife had been like. So there and then I christened her in my own mind as Messalina. I wanted to keep the name of Helga Bamberg at mental arm's length for the present. They might be one and the same person, this Messalina and Helga Bamberg, but I was determined to hold them separate until I knew more.

I memorized every square centimetre of the picture, going over the face and its features with minute care, until I could have drawn the shape of the ear, the eye, or any other part. This process I repeated with the driver of the cart.

Then there was the label: LA MARQUISE DE BRINVILLIERS

CONDUITE AU SUPPLICE, PARIS, LE 16 JUILLET 1676. PAR
JEAN REDEL. I had never heard of Jean Redel.

At last I had seen and memorized enough. I turned to my
companion and thanked him. "I think I should give you my
card, in case you may wish to check my identity," I said.
Then we parted.

As I walked away from this torchlight assignation with
Messalina, a curious feeling took possession of me. Somewhere deep in my mind there was a slow but perceptible
movement of molecules in my memory. I imagined I could
hear them bumping together, becoming more mobile and
colliding more actively. Soon, I was sure, some memory trace
would emerge into my consciousness. Messalina certainly
reminded me of something or somebody in my own past.

I went back to the Hotel George V, where Caroline and
Anne were staying, and told them I had seen the picture.
Caroline was a little calmer, though still deeply disturbed;
but I think she felt more protected. I asked her if she would
like me to stay in the same hotel; she said no, so long as I
was in Paris she felt all right. So I gave her a new supply of
sedative tablets and told her I would be along, American
fashion, to a late breakfast.

I took my baggage and moved into my usual hotel, the
Meurice, where I immediately booked a call to George Cayley. After that I rang up a friend of mine, Philippe Duclos,
who knew most of the art world of Paris, both academic and
avant-garde. I asked him if he knew of an artist called Jean
Redel and described his unusual subjects. Duclos had never
heard of him, but promised, at my urgent request, to ring
round to a few of his friends and ask them. If none of them

knew the name, the artist Jean Redel could be said not to exist in any respectable or even disreputable form.

Then I settled down to unpack, and afterwards lay on my bed to wait, and to wonder where I had seen Messalina before. In order to let my unconscious do its own research work I took out my little travelling copy of Sir Thomas Browne and began to read his luscious and relaxing prose. I had just reached his tantalizing note on the Maid of Germany, "that lived without meat upon the smell of a rose," when George Cayley came through.

"Bosch," I said unnecessarily. "It's that woman again, George. Caroline saw her today, but not in the flesh; in a picture. I've had a good look at that picture—by the light of a torch and in the company of a suspicious policeman—and I now have two problems on my mind. For somewhere I too have seen that woman or her double. The painting is a recent one and shows that nasty seventeenth-century poisoning lady, the Marquise de Brinvilliers. Our quarry posed for the Marquise, or so Caroline says—and she says it with absolute certainty. The artist is someone I've never heard of, a Jean Redel; but there are hundreds of these competent academic painters of whom nobody ever hears. I have rung a friend of mine here, and he is making inquiries."

George Cayley asked how Caroline was, and I told him she was better than I had feared, but nevertheless in a poor state.

"What bothers me, George," I continued, "is that I feel I ought to stay here and run this thing to earth; and yet I don't want Caroline to stay in Paris even if the whole thing is a fantasy. I must say I think there is some sort of flesh and blood behind it all somewhere. I think I shall ask the Langleys on Lake Garda to put up Anne and Caroline. Nellie is a dear and would, I'm sure, love looking after them both. Caroline can also sharpen her wits on George when he's not working. What do you think?"

He agreed it was a good idea, but asked me to hold up all arrangements for a day or two to see if by any chance we unearthed something quickly. If it looked like a long chase I could pack the girls off to Garda, perhaps taking them there myself, and at least have a day or two's holiday.

I sent for a light meal and then undressed. As I sat up in bed eating salmon and drinking a fine dry Chablis, I allowed my mind again to contemplate our Messalina. But again I arrived nowhere. It is no use trying to importune one's unconscious, so I let it alone once more; but I remained troubled and thwarted.

Just as I was about to lie back and try to sleep, Philippe Duclos came on the line. Only one of the four friends he had rung had ever heard of Redel, and he knew only that the man painted morbid scenes; he had not met him. Philippe also said he had checked in two dictionaries of modern artists, but without success.

"Do you think, Philippe, that it is some terribly respectable veteran of the Salon, painting under another name and supplying the morbidity market?" This idea had only that moment occurred to me.

"It could well be, Paul; and even the dealer would not know. Then again, the man the dealer thinks is Redel might himself be a middleman. If I were playing that game I would not only work under a pseudonym, but would certainly have a go-between. Wouldn't you?"

This opened up new possibilities and might lead us all on

51

an interminable wild-goose chase. I thanked Philippe for his hard work and lay back in bed with a new feeling of bafflement. Tomorrow I would go back to the Galerie Houdon and see what I could find out. But whatever happened, I decided not to make any comment on the art world's ignorance of Jean Redel.

I turned off the bedside light and repeated out loud that lovely sonnet by Keats on sleep. I found it, as Sir Thomas Browne would say, an excellent "dormative to take to bedward."

4

Next morning I found Caroline looking almost cheerful and told her that I was going to pay another visit to the picture, in daylight. I did not add that I really wanted to ask the proprietor of the Galerie Houdon who Jean Redel was. I was still no further with my unconscious, which was refusing to hand over any clue to the identity of Messalina.

I walked to the rue Bonaparte this time and enjoyed the sight of the spring frocks and, occasionally, some of the figures and faces they graced. I turned into the street with a sudden feeling of expectancy, like a bloodhound nearing his quarry. But the first blow struck me when I caught sight of the shop. One glance told me the picture had gone. Perhaps it is inside, I thought.

A thick black carpet swallowed the sound of footsteps inside the Galerie Houdon. The shop was a cleverly arranged parlour for erotico-sentimental flies. There was no vulgar ostentation in the manner of display, but the few pictures—which occupied an easel apiece—were as vulgar in themselves as they very well could be. A dull red figured wallpaper added to the general air of seduction. As I walked slowly down the aisle of easels—one could see immediately that the Brinvilliers was not amongst them—I passed in succession a corner of Old Paris, a reclining nude (very plump) on a couch (very plushy), a study of Napoleon thinking, more

Old Paris, another nude (standing), the façade of Notre Dame, another nude (propped up by what looked like an 1850 gasolier), then—

"Can I help Monsieur?"

"Oh!" I said, a little taken aback. The voice had come from a thin woman who must have silently emerged from one of the three doors I now saw at the back of the shop. She reminded me of Dracula's wife in a soap opera, but was probably in private life an excellent helpmeet and mother. She leaned forward very slightly—ready, one felt, for any slightly indecent contingency.

"Well, yes, Mam'zelle, I came to see a picture which was in your window last night—a picture of the Marquise de Brinvilliers, by Jean Redel. I hope it has not been sold." Her eyes were glancing all over me, presumably to assess my financial possibilities.

"Alas, Monsieur, yes. It was sold first thing this morning; but"—here she went on rapidly—"we have an excellent selection upstairs. There are all sorts of historical subject-pieces."

"What a pity. I particularly wanted to see that picture; but perhaps you have other works by Redel?"

"Alas, again, no. But I am sure Monsieur would like our selection." She was retreating slowly and silently backwards over the black carpet. I had no intention of following her, so she had to come forward again. I began to dislike her in spite of the wife-and-mother theory.

"Perhaps you would be good enough to tell me who bought the picture; I am sure the owner would let me see it."

There was another *"Hélas,"* another *"Non, Monsieur,"* a fluttering motion of her right hand, and her mouth began to open—I was sure—for another invitation upstairs.

54

"I think I had better see the manager," I said before she could speak.

"I fear the manager is not available." Again the motion of the right hand.

"Well, have you any good picture of a woman having her head chopped off?" I shot at her, ogre-fashion, staring at her right eye. That succeeded.

She almost ran for the door and disappeared. I was left alone with Old Paris and the nudes for a minute or two. Then a small shrewd-faced weasel of a man emerged, padded silently up to me, and bowed.

"I am Alexis Joubert, Monsieur, at your service. What was it Monsieur desired? My assistant could not quite understand."

"I particularly want to see that picture of La Brinvilliers you had in your window last night," I said rather irritably. "What is more, I am prepared to pay handsomely either to see it or to be told the address of the person who bought it this morning. Surely it cannot have left the premises."

"Indeed, Monsieur, it has left us. And I fear it would be impossible to divulge the name of the purchaser. But is it the subject matter"—here he coughed and lowered his head, but kept his eyes on me all the time—"or the artist which interests Monsieur?"

"It is the artist, Monsieur Joubert. Surely you have something else by him? I am particularly interested in his work."

The proprietor of the Galerie Houdon now took a more confidential line. "I will be frank with you, Monsieur. I have no other works by Jean Redel because each work by him is sold almost as soon as it arrives here. I place them in the window only as a matter of prestige."

"Well, can I commission the artist to paint a particular subject? Through you, of course," I added hastily.

He was looking sad now, and moving his head from side to side. "I do not want to disappoint Monsieur, but both your requests are quite impossible. Let me explain frankly. Monsieur Redel paints a particular kind of picture"—here he raised his eyebrows and almost dissociated himself from Monsieur Redel—"a kind of picture not perhaps usual, but in great demand. That demand only I, Alexis Joubert, can fulfil, because I am the sole agent of the artist. Also the artist is of a retiring disposition and does not like being worried. Now, I am being very frank with you, Monsieur, there are two or three clients who clamour for his works. Those clients pay me well, exceedingly well, and so I share the works amongst them. But I am not at liberty to disclose their names, Monsieur; definitely not."

What on earth, I wondered, was I up against now? I asked him what he meant by a "particular kind of picture," and did this refer to *"quelque chose d'érotique?"* I had visions of three rich and naughty old men trying to outbid each other, without even knowing who their competitors were, for elaborately painted nudes, or even worse.

"Ah, that I can tell you, Monsieur, because after all I always put them in my window for a day or two when they arrive. No, they are not especially erotic, although I suppose there is always that element in them. Most of the works, Monsieur, show scenes of violence, of executions, murders, and the like." My unconscious gave me another prod; I felt my memory groping anew. My facetious question to Mrs. Dracula seemed oddly prophetic now.

56

"And most, if not all, of the victims are women?" I put in, prompted by some vague stirring of memory.

"Monsieur is having a joke with me—he has obviously seen the works of Monsieur Redel." He looked at me crossly.

"No, as a matter of fact I haven't," I replied, "but it rather follows from what you say. I am a psychiatrist and am concerned with such things. I am particularly interested at the moment, as I have a patient in England, a very rich patient, who is probably like your clients. I want very much to purchase one of these pictures, or at least a photograph of one, to show him and get his reactions." It was a lame enough story, but he seemed suddenly to be more friendly, and for a curious reason, which he then revealed.

"Ah, Monsieur, you are a psychiatrist. My sister, she was very ill and was completely cured by a psychiatrist, a Dr. Meusnier here in Paris. I wish I could help you. In the matter of my clients and the commission, I cannot; but perhaps I could secure some photographs for you."

I knew Meusnier, and I told him so; Meusnier, like myself, was very interested in criminal psychology. My initial distaste for Alexis Joubert began to pale under the stress of expediency. I now appeared to have a new friend in the art dealer, if I wanted him. His manner had undergone a complete transformation.

"Tell me," I said, "does Jean Redel often include that handsome, imperious sort of woman in his pictures?"

"Oh, indeed, she occurs in very many of them. She is his favourite model. A remarkable thing, Monsieur—I have never seen the lady; and my friends in the trade, they have never seen her either, although Redel lives in Paris. And he is such a skinny one, that Jean Redel. But so it goes, does it not? That kind of man often worships the statuesque type, does he not? But Monsieur Redel, he always slaughters them in his pictures—that is strange, is it not?"

I felt that it would do no good to say that the skinny Jean Redel was probably quite an ambivalent character in his odd way; but I was about to make a polite comment when Joubert continued, "To give you an idea of the kind of thing my clients pay so well for, the last painting but one was typical. It showed the execution of Hieronyma Spara, her assistant, and three noble ladies, in Rome in 1660 or thereabouts. It was, I believe, another famous poison case in which they got rid of their husbands with a secret poison provided by La Spara. The picture was terrible, Monsieur, but I am told it was historically correct. The women were being hanged in public, and they were all stripped naked to the waist, having first been whipped through the streets. The centre of the picture was taken up by the ringleader herself, who was already hanging from the gallows. The other ladies were seen behind her, two hanging and the others being got ready. I need scarcely tell you that the main figure was Jean Redel's favourite model." He paused. "I think I might be able to get you a photograph of that one."

I thanked him, and then something struck me. "Monsieur Joubert, you seem well up in your history. I suppose your clients demand full details about the subjects they buy?"

"It is odd that you ask me that," he said. "It is as you say; at the outset they asked me about the subjects, and of course I didn't know a thing about them. To tell the truth, Redel's pictures rather horrified me at the beginning, but I've got used to them now. After all, I prefer my women alive, and not such formidable figures as the madame he paints. However, I told him he must produce details of what he depicted, and now a typewritten description comes with each picture. I keep copies of all of them in my order book, and I will show them to you one day if you like. But I must cover up the payments I received," he concluded with a smile.

I thanked him, gave him my card with the name of the hotel added—that seemed to please him too—and said I would call in to have another chat with him soon. I also asked him to send the photograph if he could get one.

Walking back to my lunch appointment with Caroline and Anne, I again suffered acutely from the sense of frustrated memory. A psychiatrist relies a great deal on his memory, and it becomes trained by practice to a remarkable degree. Most of us can remember the dreams and experiences, and even individual remarks, of our patients for years back. It was this fact that settled one point for me. Whatever it was I was trying to remember could not, I thought, have involved one of my own patients. It would almost certainly have come back to me in an instant. No; it was something I must have heard, and not very recently.

After a rather subdued lunch—Caroline was depressed again—at which I only touched on my visit to the Galerie Houdon, I took her to the Louvre. Anne was off to see some friends, and we were all to meet for cocktails at Fouquet's. Caroline said she wanted to see the Italians, and it turned out we both had a special favourite amongst them—Fra Angelico's "Coronation of the Virgin." We stood a long time in front of it, neither of us speaking, and it seemed to impose upon both of us a profound calm. The eye moves so gracefully over the kneeling saints in the foreground and then triumphantly mounts the steps, to rest finally on the figure of the Virgin, with her long train sweeping up to the folded hands and the serene face.

As we walked away from it, Caroline bent her head forward a little, and I knew she was going to say something diffident but personal.

"How can you take such pleasure in that picture if you don't believe in the Christian faith?" she asked.

"I have never said I disbelieved, Caroline. As a matter of fact I am sometimes a theist, sometimes an agnostic, but never an atheist. And in any case the deep and universal appeal of such pictures, their serenity of harmonies—or harmony of serenities—can surely appeal beyond morals and beliefs and dogmas."

"I see," she said after a minute. "I suppose that may be so. Apart from its wonderful peace and beauty, I think it is the colour that casts its spell over one at first. I remember how one French author described it—'tous ces bienheureux sont baignés d'une céleste et chantante couleur.'"

We were moving aimlessly round the galleries, and Caroline seemed to be enjoying herself as her eyes roamed from picture to picture. She was looking particularly lovely today, in a simple lime-green frock; her hair was swept up in a pile on top, and now and then she made that slight ducking movement of her head when talking, which had its own peculiar charm. We had come into the French rooms, and Caroline had stopped to look at Corot's famous "Souvenir de Mortefontaine," which she thought sentimental. I had left her in front of it and wandered off to the other side of the gallery. I found myself gazing with distaste at that grotesque but oddly competent picture by Decamps called "Le Singe

60

Peintre." It is always popular with the tourists, and shows a monkey sitting on the floor painting a picture which is leaning against an old chest; on the wall behind hang a palette, an old shotgun of some sort, and a porcelain-bowled pipe.

Then the single word "monkey" came echoing back to me as if from the end of a long tunnel. But only the word came, charged with feeling, but prompting no associations. It was a madly tantalizing moment. "Monkey-monkey-monkey-monkey," I repeated to myself. Where on earth had I met that word in some special context? Another little fragment then flew to me from out of the black tunnel. "Monkey" had been the nickname—no, the code-name—for a man. That was it; a code-name. But what man? When? Where?

"Oh, bloody hell!" I said, as I thought, to myself.

"Dr. Harvard, that is the first time I have ever heard you swear." I turned round with a start. She was not a bit shocked; she was standing there smiling, almost as if she had caught me out in some mild indiscretion.

"I'm afraid I must get back to my hotel. Do you mind if we go now?"

"Not a bit," she said, now viewing me with evident concern. "Do you feel unwell?"

I realized then that I must have seemed strange to her during the last minute or two.

"Unwell? Oh heavens, no. I have just thought of something which I must ask George Cayley urgently, that's all," I said.

Caroline cast one disapproving, yet inquisitive, look at the monkey picture as we made off hurriedly down the great echoing gallery.

5

I left Caroline at her hotel and walked quickly down the rue de Rivoli to the Meurice. I wanted only to get hold of George Cayley. The call to London took an unconscionably long time, and I paced my room like a caricature lion. At last the hotel switchboard rang me and said London had come through.

"Mary," I barked across the Channel, "I want Sir George urgently. Is he available?"

"You're coming over very loud, Dr. Harvard. Yes, you're lucky, he's in." Then the calm voice of George Cayley asked, "How are you, Paul? What can we do for you?"

"I am trying to calm down, George, but this wretched business has been getting rather on my nerves. First, can I see you tomorrow, about eleven? Second, have you any information about a certain species of *monkey?*" I heavily accentuated the word.

"Yes to both questions. I know quite a lot about the animal and am very interested in its habits. See you at eleven. How is Caroline?"

I said she was reasonably well and that she could be left for a little.

After I had hung up the receiver I lay down on my bed. I was suddenly more composed, and the reason was that Cayley might see a way through the maze I was in. My "monkey" clue obviously meant something to him. Now, for a change, I could look forward instead of back. I flew over to London early next morning, reaching Northolt at ten.

When I arrived at George Cayley's Whitehall office an hour later I was again feeling irked and thwarted, and decided I must soon be having a few days' holiday. I don't mind moving quickly about the world, but I had done rather too much of it lately and wanted time to collect my wits. Also, I was more than usually put out about the Caroline case. She would cooperate with me only when she felt seriously ill. If she had not been one of Cayley's "specials," and —let me admit—if she had not invaded a peculiarly private part of my own being, I should have refused to go on with the case and recommended her to some dear old doctor who would be fatherly and provide an Abrahamic bosom for her to rest upon when she wanted. But Caroline had indeed invaded one of my fenced zones, and I knew I would go to the ends of the earth for her if I thought it would do her any good.

I heard the door shut behind the discreet old messenger, and stood facing that calm and efficient man I worked for.

"Well, Paul," he greeted me, "what develops now, and where have you come across Monkey?" His smooth round face was suffused by a smile which said clearly enough that he knew I was upset and was willing to do all he could to stand me upright again.

"I wish to heaven I could see my way more clearly, George. Two weeks ago I was trying to cure a very remarkable but not very cooperative young woman. Now I'm involved with invisible artists, invisible women, a still uncured

63

and still uncooperative Caroline, and finally an inaccessible memory connected with a monkey."

I first of all gave him an account of what had happened in Paris, up to the moment I had stood in front of the monkey-artist picture. "Then, George, something hit me— the word 'monkey'; and for the life of me I could not batter anything out of my memory except a conviction that it was someone's code-name."

"It *was* someone's code-name, and we are even now quite worried about the business. You must have met the name when dealing with 'Mark' when we had him back in rather a bad state—you remember him, of course." Indeed I remembered, and now the word "monkey" was meaning quite a lot to me.

"Monkey," continued Cayley, "was one of our men in Germany, whose cover occupation was painting. He was a remarkable man—perhaps the most remarkable person we had there at that time. He had lived in the country for many years and had become almost a German in everything but loyalty. He acted as a communication centre and specialized in sending out material provided by other agents which could not be passed on by radio or by other rapid means. He was actually a professional artist, and subsequently we managed to establish an agent for him in Brussels. The pictures were sent there, and an ingenious method was devised for conveying the material in a lined canvas, which, incidentally, could then be read only by infra-red rays when one knew where to look. The lining canvas was soaked off by the agent and retained, and the innocent picture went on to its destination. I expect some of these details are coming back to you.

"The agent then succeeded in interesting a harmless old German general who was in an Occupation job near Brussels. He had a secret passion for sadistic pictures, but they had, so to speak, to be respectable. It was this demand which Monkey himself delighted in supplying. He had always been a puzzle to us. Ugly, rather like a monkey himself, he was the gentlest and kindest person one could imagine. He got on with everyone, and was, of course, invaluable to us over the years. But he had some quirk about women—although he seemed to like them well enough—which came out in his pictures. For his favourite subjects were females, generally historical characters, undergoing torture or execution. The agent in Brussels said he had never seen anything like them; picture after picture arrived, meticulously painted, showing these unfortunate creatures in every state of undress and in every kind of extremity. A peculiar feature of the later pictures was the presence of the same model for the chief figure in almost every work—a handsome but aggressive woman. This combination of sex and savagery found a ready market; and when the old general arrived on the scene it became a nearly perfect set-up. We got the pictures out of Germany more easily, and it was also more satisfactory for them all to go to one insatiable customer. I expect, Paul, that you will have an explanation for both the supplier and the demander."

Now my memory was complete. My patient "Mark" had once given me a most vivid account of some of these paintings and of their central character. It was my vivid imagination of what I had been told that had found an echo in the Redel picture. But I was very interested in Cayley's story of this morbid but comparatively harmless artist—fantasy sadists being almost always kind to real women and animals. I asked what had happened to Monkey.

"Now comes the mystery," he went on, "for Monkey suddenly stopped sending his pictures to Brussels. The agent there, of course, notified us, and he started checking through various channels. But no trace of Monkey could be found. He was known to have left his Munich flat, but after that there was a blank. It was obvious to us that the Abwehr had caught him; but mercifully the Brussels agent changed his skin in time. There was, as you know, a standing danger period; and no matter what accidents might have occurred to delay the signals, it meant at least temporary disappearance at once. If it were a false alarm, well and good. But in this case the Germans raided our agent's flat in Brussels the day after he had left. What rather interested me was a vague suggestion, which came through one of the wicked brethren —the fellows who played on both sides and thought we didn't know—that Monkey had gone over to the enemy. But if that had been true, our people would certainly have suffered somewhere else along the chain. And they hadn't." He paused. "Now, I wonder where all this fits in with what you have told me. There is something most peculiar about the whole business."

"George, I feel certain that we are on to something. I can only hope it is something that will help Caroline. It is surely more than a coincidence that we have not only the same set-up in the case of Jean Redel, but with the interesting fact that the lady in question is not seen about in Paris; we have Joubert's word for that. And there is also something rather odd about Redel himself. Few people seem to have heard of him either. I telephoned a friend of mine in Paris,

66

Philippe Duclos, who knows everyone in the art world, both advanced and academic; he had never heard of Redel, and only one of the various friends he rung up had ever heard tell of him, and even then only vaguely. That, of course, proves nothing, I know. But the pictures and the model—they must add up to something, I should have thought."

George Cayley sat in silence, looking down at the clean blotter in front of him. I could imagine his acute and tidy mind flashing over every fact and facet of the Monkey case, sorting, weighing, and comparing.

I lay back in the big green armchair and felt relaxed for the first time that day. I had shared my burden, and I felt lighter for the action. I lazily examined the office we were in, a typical senior civil servant's working place—cream and green, with a big desk, carpet, three armchairs, and a tall safe in the corner by the window. But there were no papers, no books, no paraphernalia of any kind, except a large pink blotter and three telephones of different colours—black, green, and red.

We sat silent for exactly six and a half minutes—I timed it by the mantelpiece clock—and the Whitehall traffic beyond the window supplied the only noise that came to us. Then Cayley lifted the black telephone and asked his secretary to come in. She came at once, a tall, well-preserved, and well-tailored woman in her fifties, and quietly shut the heavy door behind her.

"Susan, I want you to go and fetch John, Albert, and Ronald. Tell them it will take a little time."

I wondered if these purposely surnameless individuals would be able to help, because George Cayley gave me the feeling that his long train of thought had led him nowhere.

He said as much after Susan had left. "I don't know quite what to make of it. There is, of course, no theoretical reason why Monkey should not be alive; but to go on painting his pictures when he must know we might see them at some time would be absurd—absurd, that is to say, if he didn't want us to know he was alive. And a deliberate anonymity is the only tenable theory if he is not dead. But what you say is certainly strange, very strange indeed. We shall see if our trio has any ideas; they were all concerned with Monkey in one way or another."

At that point they came in, all together. They were the most studiously colourless men imaginable. I had seen one of them before, and we nodded to each other. I was idly classifying them in my mind: John was tall and thin (J is a tall thin letter); Albert was reasonably bulky (so is the roundly written capital A); and Ronald was my previous acquaintance, except that he had not then been "Ronald." I was introduced, and they sat down, Ronald perching on the arm of Albert's chair.

"Gentlemen, this is Dr. Harvard—you may have met. You all know about the Monkey case. Dr. Harvard has come across something very peculiar which may have a bearing on it. He is at present looking after Caroline Norton, and I think, Paul, you might give them a brief sketch of the Caroline case to start with. Then go ahead and tell them in detail what you have just told me."

So I outlined the story of Caroline as it touched me, and then again went over the new developments in Paris, paying attention to the smallest details I remembered, or even thought I remembered.

Ronald was the first to speak. "The subjects, Sir George;

they were definitely among the Belgian consignments. It is very odd. I cannot see how it fits, but I agree with Dr. Harvard that something ought to fit."

"What about the original pictures?" I asked. "If I could see some of them, I think I am enough of a critic to tell if they were done by the same hand."

"Do you mean that, Paul?" asked George Cayley. "Is it really possible to tell such things? I know, of course, that you can tell the different painters amongst the great. But suppose these are very similar, do you think you could differentiate between them?"

"Quite likely, I think; but in any case I could lay on a dozen people who could do it even better than I could."

"Well, that is the first thing we shall have to do—locate those pictures if they still survive and are not dispersed all over Europe. Wait." He paused. "Paul, I have just thought of something; so have you, by your expression. What if that Belgian stock has been dispersed, and this Redel person had his hands on them? What would be easier than to parcel them out, one by one, and pretend they were his. It would be easy to sign them, wouldn't it?"

That was just what I too had been considering as he spoke. Then I had another idea. "What," I asked, "was Monkey's German name, under which he presumably painted?"

"Leder," said Albert. At that word another switch was thrown in my mind, and I almost started out of my chair.

"Don't you see, George, L-e-d-e-r; spell it backwards."

"Well, I'll be damned," said George Cayley, and it was a very uncharacteristic expression for him.

It was John who now leaned forward. "It still doesn't rule out the possibility of Redel having the pictures and reversing the name. I think, Sir George, we had better signal Brussels and see if they can help. Do you agree?"

"Yes; tell them to do everything they can and as fast as they can. Until then, Paul, we must be patient. And another thing. Ronald, did we never know anything about this model of Leder's, this large aggressive woman that Dr. Harvard has christened Messalina? We will adopt that name until further notice, by the way."

"No, Sir George, we knew nothing about her. Only that she appeared comparatively late in Monkey's career. I don't think she was there much before what we might call the Brussels period. That might of course mean anything. She might just have happened along as a model and taken his fancy as such—she obviously did just that. Before that, if I remember rightly, there were always rather 'Roman matron' types in the pictures, but not one particular woman. But I've never seen the pictures. I only know, or think I know, from that meticulous report—you remember, Sir George— that our man there sent over after he had got the route working well. I remember him commenting on the appearance of this one apparently favourite model."

After the trio had left, George Cayley and I walked across the Horse Guards Parade and had a late lunch at the Athenæum. As we sat upstairs in the library drinking our coffee we discussed Caroline, and we again talked about sending her to Garda if the Langleys would have her and Anne, which I was sure they would. I said I would like her well out of the way and in completely peaceful surroundings until we had cleared up the Messalina business, if indeed it could ever be cleared up.

"You see, George, there are so many 'ifs.' If there is a

70

Messalina alive now—in other words, if Helga is alive—Caroline may run into her, although it's very unlikely. If, on the other hand, we can prove she is dead, it *may* have some effect on Caroline. At present she is suspended, so to say, between a fantasy and a reality. Helga was once alive and did torture her—no matter where our lady devil is now —and, although Caroline brought that incredibly painful incident up under ether, it did not completely exorcise Helga. So now she knows all about the Helga of reality, but also preserves a fantasy Helga of whom she is still terrified, and of whose present living existence she is irrationally convinced.

"If Caroline were not so unbending psychologically, and if only she would cooperate, I might get it all out of her. But she won't cooperate. Therefore we must face up to the fact that she may carry this bogy about inside her forever, unless we can produce evidence that satisfies her fantasy belief, and that is a very unlikely achievement. She may, however, have a relapse and be forced to cooperate out of sheer necessity. But until I see daylight somewhere, I think she must rest in the most peaceful and secluded surroundings. From what I told her about the Langley ménage at Garda, she seemed to like the idea."

So we decided it should be Garda for Caroline, and I rang Paris that afternoon. I told her I would be back in a day or two, and that I would still "lend" her Anne if she would go to Garda. She was clearly delighted at this, and I said I would take them both to the Langleys', spend a few days there myself if I could, and then come back and search for Helga. She was also pleased at the idea of my searching for her devil, as it seemed to her that if I were engaged in locating Helga, Helga was less likely to be a menace to her. I knew, and she knew I knew, that this was her fantasy fear speaking; but we both knew it was a painful enough fear and must be dealt with. I promised I would always come out to Garda if she had a bad attack of anxiety, but the whole set-up there appeared sufficiently protective for her in her present mood. I then repeated the whole scheme to Anne, and after nearly half an hour on the line I put down the telephone in George Cayley's office.

"Now I'm going to find a good Western movie, and then home to bed," I said. And we parted for the day.

6

The Wild West film took me successfully out of the world of officialdom and psychopathology; it was a coloured affair of wonderful scenery and much banditry, and I returned home to the Porchester in a better frame of mind. I was pleased to see the calm face of Sarah in the hall of my flat, and we walked arm in arm across the library and stood looking out over the park and talking about the weather. Then she remembered something.

"Oh dear, Mr. Paul, I forgot. A few letters have come for you—I think you should see one of them especially. It is marked 'Urgent' and was sent on from Wimpole Street this afternoon. I'll go and get it." It struck me in passing that an urgent letter passed on from Wimpole Street was odd. All officially urgent letters would, of course, have come via George Cayley, and the few patients I was treating had a very good and kindly colleague of mine in Harley Street to look after them.

Sarah brought the small pile of letters, mostly bills and circulars, with the urgent one on top. I picked it up and turned it over carefully by force of habit, examining every mark and detail. (In one of the curious courses Cayley had made me take years ago I had learned a lot about letters.) I opened it and read it.

Mangrave Hall
Wimborne
Dorset

DEAR SIR,

I should be glad if you would leave a message at the United Service Club giving a time for me to see you. Any time within the next five days will suit me. I would rather not mention the nature of my business in a letter, but it is urgent, and it is important that I see you as soon as possible.

Yours faithfully,
DENNIS M. NEWCOMEN
(Col. Sir D. M. Newcomen, Bt.)

P.S. On second thoughts, and in case you might consider this to be some communication from a would-be patient, I had better say that my business concerns Miss Caroline Norton.

I had never heard of Sir Dennis Newcomen, who so thoughtfully provided both his title and his military rank, but of course the address struck me immediately. It was near Wimborne; so also was Caroline's home. Could this, I wondered, be the man whom Cayley had casually mentioned as living near by and being fond of Caroline? I felt sure it was.

I went over to the telephone and dialled a number, catching sight as I did so of a small picture of St. George and the Dragon which I had picked up in Munich before the war. I smiled and thought it might be prophetic—myself, of course, in the role of the dragon.

I got through to George Cayley and read him the letter and asked what he knew about Newcomen.

"Precious little, Paul, but I think he is the man who likes our lady. I have heard her parents speak of him, and I seem to remember his being treated as rather a favourite. Go

74

ahead and see him and find out what it's all about. Meanwhile I'll have details of him looked up and sent round to you early tomorrow morning."

"You know, I don't much like seeing this man until I have Caroline's permission. It is rigid etiquette in our line of business never to discuss a patient, no matter how briefly, with anyone without the patient's permission. Do you mind if I ring up Caroline and simply say that Newcomen has appeared on the scene and wants to see me? And what, by the way, shall my story to Newcomen consist of?"

"Yes, I had forgotten about that for the moment. Certainly you had better ring her. But say that I should like her to agree to your seeing him because I want him reassured and stopped as a possible interference. I will think up a story for you and put it in my note."

"One other thing, George; would you mind coping with the parents and telling them whatever you think best?" George Cayley promised, and we rang off.

My attempt to telephone Caroline in Paris failed, as she was out with Anne, so I left an urgent message for her to ring me when she came in. I had nearly two hours to wait before she rang, and it was a troubled voice which asked what was wrong.

"Nothing's wrong, Caroline, but something important has come up. A Colonel Sir Dennis Newcomen has by some means found out that you are seeing me and has demanded an interview. Now I shall not see him at all if you refuse your permission. But I have talked to Sir George, and he suggests it is better if I do see him and find out what he has to say. Then I can tell him a semi-fake story, which Sir George is thinking up now, and we can stop him if he is

75

going round asking a lot of questions and talking to your parents. What do you think?"

"Dennis Newcomen is a friend and neighbour of mine, Dr. Harvard. I think he is rather fond of me, and I think he is a very nice person. I can't imagine why he should get on to you, unless—yes, I think I do know the reason—he has a poor opinion of psychiatrists, and he may feel I have to be rescued in some way. If you and Sir George think it best to see him, you must go ahead. Only let me know the story you agree on so that I can tell the same version if and when I have to."

When we had rung off I glanced again at St. George and then looked up the number of the club. When they answered, I asked if I could leave a message for Sir Dennis Newcomen, and the porter said he happened to be in the club at the moment as he was staying the night. Would I care to speak to him? I hesitated a moment, then said yes, and gave my name.

The voice that next came over the line held a curious blend of consideration—I was about to say kindness—and irritation. "This man," I said to myself, "is annoyed with me."

"Dr. Harvard? I thought I would have heard from you before. What time can you see me? I think it best if you come here."

I paused for quite a long time before I answered. "Colonel Newcomen, I will see you at my Wimpole Street consulting room at eleven-thirty tomorrow morning. That is the only time I can manage." And I rang off before he could answer. I was a little annoyed with Colonel Newcomen.

Next morning Sarah brought me a long white envelope

as I sat comfortably eating my breakfast in the library. I put it on one side, finished my egg, stretched my legs until they stuck out of my pyjamas like hairy stalks, and then opened George Cayley's bulletin. It read:

Dear Paul,

Not much, but enough for the moment I hope. He is the fifth baronet; had an excellent war record—Parachute Regiment—D.S.O., M.C. and bar; owns quite a big estate which touches the Nortons'; considerable private means, and breeds police dogs and blind-guide dogs for a hobby, which has become quite a business; a considerable expert on the Baltic region and has dealings on the subject with M.I.34, where his contact is a Colonel Mayhew; is an excellent horseman. I remember now, he is much liked by C's parents, but C's attitude to him is friendly but very reserved; age 37; very well liked in the neighbourhood as a quiet and understanding person.

He has obviously discovered she has seen you—find out how he did that and let me know—which means he has either told C's parents or may do so at any minute. If this happens I will tell them half the truth (and you can tell him the same story) and say that we can now reveal the fact that C worked with the French Resistance, was caught and had a bad time, and that you were giving her special drugs to counteract some rare infection she picked up over there and which has been troubling her off and on ever since. It has now broken out again, and she is in a low state and has gone away to recuperate.

Yours,

G.

I now looked forward to this meeting with considerable interest, and I was sitting at my desk in Wimpole Street reading an American article on hypnotism when the receptionist showed Sir Dennis Newcomen in.

Strangely enough, I took to him immediately, despite my previous irritation. He seemed very much the type of quiet man of action that part of me had secretly wished to be since I was a boy. Medium height, fair hair, very clear blue eyes, and a quiet self-possessed manner. But his curt telephone conversation of last night was echoed in his expression as he came into the room. He did not offer to shake hands, but immediately sat down in my straight-backed visitor's chair and asked in a rather over-controlled voice, "Dr. Harvard, what are you treating Miss Norton for?"

I decided I would not at first let him know that I had told Caroline of his visit. "I haven't said I am treating any Miss Norton for anything," I replied, "and even if I were, I certainly should not discuss the affairs of my patients with anyone."

"I see; so that's your line. Well, let me say this. I am not sure what is going on, and if you don't tell me now I shall take it up through certain contacts I have with the police."

I wished such an obviously nice person would not make such a fool of himself. I could have had him shown out there and then, and that would have been an end to the matter. But if he were a friend of Caroline's, and if he were fond of her, I would do what I could for him, but in my own time.

"Take *what* up?" I asked.

"You may be protected by the law, Dr. Harvard, or you may not. All I know is that Miss Norton, who is a friend and neighbour of mine, has suddenly left her home. Her parents have been told that she is engaged in some work for the Air Ministry. I have made inquiries there, and they know nothing about her, and I very regretfully told her parents

78

yesterday what I had found out. They at first did not take me seriously, as their informant was a very old friend whom they say they will ring today; and also they had heard from their daughter herself. I pointed out that anyone could counterfeit a voice, that the letter they received might have been written under duress, and that she had been seen entering and leaving this house. I told them you were a psychiatrist and that I had had enough to do with what we called 'trick-cyclists' during the war to be very suspicious of the whole thing.

"At that they were very disturbed and asked me to do what I could to find out, while they would try and get through to this man Cayley, who is apparently in some government job. It was purely by chance that I happened to see her come out of this house, but before I could reach her she and another girl got into a taxi and were gone. I marked the house, but I was prevented from making inquiries until some time later. That is why I am here, and if you will not talk, I shall, as I said, make inquiries through the police." At this he got up, but did not make for the door.

"Sir Dennis, I don't quite know what to do about you. You are obviously sincere, and I believe you are fond of Miss Norton—"

"Ah," he shot at me, "so you admit you know her."

"Now, for heaven's sake, sit down and don't be an ass; otherwise I shall get angry too. And the spectacle of two angry adults who have never heard of, or seen, each other before in their lives would be childish and unedifying. And it won't help you or Miss Norton, either. Incidentally, I wonder if Colonel Mayhew of M.I.34 knows you have such an emotionally unstable side to your character." This was

79

very pompous of me and even mean, I know; but something had to be done to bring him down to earth. It was clearly successful, for he slowly sat down and looked at me with a face in which the anger had been chased away by shocked surprise.

"That's better," I said. "Have a cigarette." Without a word we both lit up. Thank heaven that is over, I thought.

"Sir Dennis, what do you know about Miss Norton's war service?" He now looked and acted like an ordinary human being.

"As far as I know, and from what she said, she was in some sort of WAAF Intelligence job, which of course we did not discuss. That is what her parents thought too. Why? What did she do?"

"Miss Norton was attached to the WAAF as a cover. Actually she worked with the French Resistance, did magnificently, and was finally caught by the Germans."

"Caroline? With the French Resistance? And caught by the Germans?" he repeated almost in a whisper. "What on earth—? What a wonderful woman—and she never said a word; never a hint. My God, what a woman!"

It was really moving to see the admiration and affection which suddenly took possession of him. I thought to myself that I would like, perhaps grudgingly, to see that young woman marry him one day. I also wondered if Caroline knew how deeply he cared; and, if so, if she cared.

"You are in love with Miss Norton, are you not?" I asked. I was glad he did not blush or get confused.

"Yes, I suppose I am. But she has never given me the slightest encouragement." There was just a trace of bitterness in his voice. "I don't know what she thinks of me." He suddenly paused and looked up at me. "I don't know why I am telling you all this, Dr. Harvard. I came here to have a row with you, and here I am behaving like a schoolboy. But now you know what I feel, I should like to ask, if I may, how you come into this."

"I think I should tell you now that I phoned Miss Norton yesterday and received her permission to see you. Otherwise I could have told you nothing. What I am going to say you must keep to yourself at present. Sir George Cayley will tell her parents this evening. When Miss Norton was captured by the Germans she was tortured—" He drew in his breath sharply at this, and leaned forward as if to speak. But I went on. "She was terribly ill when she was rescued by the Americans. She had picked up a rare infection which has been troubling her off and on ever since, and recently she has had another attack, and we have been treating her."

"But you are a psychiatrist, aren't you? The maid here said you were, when I asked, and that is backed up by what the medical directory says."

"Psychiatrists are ordinary doctors first and psychiatrists afterwards. And incidentally this infection makes her very depressed. As I work for various government departments, they put her in my charge, and I work with another specialist on her case. At present she is abroad, resting. She is with my own secretary and is in good hands. Now are you satisfied?"

The poor man had careened round so many mental turnings since he entered my consulting room that he was now quite dizzy. "I want to apologize, Dr. Harvard. All I can say in defence of my insufferable behaviour is that I was nearly driven mad with worry about her. I am, as I told you, very fond of her; and if anything happened to her I don't know what I would do. Again, I'm terribly sorry for what I said to you."

"There is nothing to apologize or be sorry for. You couldn't have known what had happened, and neither she nor the Air Ministry people wanted it talked about. And if I may say a word on my own account, I am delighted that she has someone like yourself to look to. I sincerely hope that one day you will marry her. She is a most lovely and remarkable person. And, incidentally, I'm sorry I was rather pompous when we started this conversation."

After my visitor had closed the door behind him, I sat quietly for a minute or two before I rang George Cayley. I was thinking that now there was an added reason why we must cure Caroline Norton. I was also aware of feeling faintly jealous.

7

Next morning I had my breakfast to the accompaniment of pouring rain, and I felt particularly reluctant to leave my flat. I walked aimlessly from room to room, picking up books, looking at pictures, and staring out over Hyde Park, until forced back into the momentarily less attractive world of my work by a call from Mary. She said that George Cayley would like to see me at eleven-thirty. So I got dressed, put on a mackintosh, and walked in the rain to Whitehall, feeling that the exercise might do me good, and the rain no harm.

All the way there I had been thinking of what to do about Caroline. I would have liked to go back to Paris that evening and take her and Anne to Garda as soon as the Langleys could have us. I could then have a few days' holiday there, and wait for the news from Brussels. I could do nothing until I heard from Brussels.

When I was settled in Cayley's office I was about to put my plans to him when I realized that he was in a troubled state of mind. "You look worried," I said. "Is it anything I can know about?"

"Yes, Paul, it is very much your business, as well as mine. You remember, when we were at Scotland Yard with Caroline, I said that something had arisen which might make it essential for Caroline to go back into harness for a bit?" I nodded. "Well, that business has boiled up into a vitally important issue. Caroline has now become of extreme importance to us. We had a meeting this morning at which various alternatives were discussed—alternative operatives, I should say, in view of Caroline's being ill. But it was the unanimous feeling that we should wait and see if you get her well enough to take on this assignment.

"I will give you a few more details to show you how uncomfortably important she has now become. This man whom I mentioned is almost certainly what we feared—a central figure in an international group which both the French and ourselves view with considerable alarm. The man lives in a fair-sized provincial town in France where he is ostensibly a librarian—a job he apparently asked for and received after his fine Resistance record. His previous history is oddly nebulous, but bits and pieces are slowly coming to light, and they add up to something formidable.

"Now Caroline, as I said, was the object of considerable attention from this man, which of course she dealt with in her usual manner. But she has already—with our blessing —been to one of the Resistance reunions in this town, although she did not much like the visit. We had not this particular man in mind at the time, but those Resistance groups included some strange types. We thought it would do no harm to have one of our own people keep in touch with them. So Caroline promised to go back again. It would now be a godsend for us if she could keep that promise."

"When is the next reunion?" I asked.

"In December of this year."

We both sat and thought about Caroline for some minutes, Cayley with hope and expectation, I with fear and uncertainty.

"George," I said suddenly, "how about Caroline knowing about you now—I mean in case she slips up and gets into trouble? I know there is less risk in peacetime, but surely there is danger of her being made to talk?"

"We discussed that quite fully at the meeting. It was decided that she is so essential for the task that she must risk it—with precautions, of course. We remembered her fake story when she was tortured, and we are going to tell her to give way slowly on the identity of a man at present in the Foreign Office who will be known to them, but as a matter of fact has nothing to do with us. If my name specifically is brought up she can't tell them much as she knows nothing much, and today it wouldn't matter—if it came to the worst —if they knew I was in the game. They wouldn't be much the wiser. Then finally we will give her a new variation of that poison capsule—just for extreme emergencies."

I shuddered. I had seen those poison capsules in action. I said nothing.

"From now on, Paul, I am putting all our official facilities at your disposal. The first practical move I have made—and I hope you approve—is to appoint an assistant for you. His name is James Montgomery—an admirable young man. I think you once met him. He will be able to meet you, let's say in Paris, in a week's time."

"Well, that will be a considerable help straight away, and I could ask for no one better." Then I told him my immediate plans for Caroline and myself, with which he agreed.

"It would be a tragic piece of misfortune if you cannot have her right before the winter," he said. "What about

85

telling her how important it is for us that she gets well soon? Would that be wise?"

"No, I don't think I would tell her if I were you. It would bring into play her strong sense of duty, and there would then be yet another conflict raging inside her. I would rather do without that for the moment, if you don't mind. In any case, if we can really use the Department for all it's worth, it will be a great help, and will speed things up all round, I hope."

"Well, Paul, I know you will do your utmost. But now for our immediate moves. The more I think of the whole business, the more I am convinced that something very curious is going on. As a start I have decided on a cover story for you all which will satisfy the French and Belgian police, and anybody else whom we have to involve abroad. We will tell the International Drug Control people, through Scotland Yard, that in investigating a case of forgery you believe you have a line on a new drug route. We can play one story off against the other for long enough, I hope, to give us time to finish our business."

"I think that is an excellent idea," I said.

"You know, I'm getting more and more worried about the effect of all this on Caroline as a person, quite apart from her usefulness to the Service. Let me try and see things straight, by framing some questions. Just suppose Messalina-Helga is alive, quite apart from Monkey; then what are we to do? Equally, what are we to do if she is proved to be dead? If Caroline thinks she is alive, and if she is in fact dead, it is necessary—if I remember you rightly—to bring some exceptionally strong evidence to convince Caroline. Even then, her fantasy belief in Helga's existence might be too strong to be battered down by facts. That will be a terrible problem for you and for me. If we discover Helga alive, I doubt if we could get any action under way to have her imprisoned as a war criminal. In any case she would still be alive, even in prison, and hence a possible threat to Caroline."

He looked up at me with some peculiarly tight lines around his mouth.

"I wish to goodness we could stage a re-enactment of one of Monkey's pictures," he said. "But in peacetime such a thing is out of the question. So it is up to you to solve the problem as best you can. Do you think Caroline could somehow be reconciled to a live Helga-Messalina?"

The pause before I gave my answer to the last question was occupied with a sudden determination to take that matter into my own hands if necessary, without even hinting to Cayley what I had in mind.

"It is possible, yes," I replied. "It might even be feasible to bring them face to face. A frightening reality is always better than a terrifying fantasy. And what Caroline is suffering from, whether Helga is alive or dead, is still a fantasy fear. We might at least try and convert that into a reality fear which we could help her to face and deal with. After all, she has faced far worse reality situations before in her life."

My secret thought had hardened. If Helga Bamberg was alive and could be found, I would kill her if it could help Caroline. I would have no compunction at all. It did not even seem a difficult decision to make now, in view of what was at stake—Caroline's health first, and then the job Cayley had outlined to me. I believed I knew just how dangerous

87

that Frenchman might be, not only to his own country, but to Europe. I suddenly realized Cayley was speaking.

"By the way, James Montgomery will bring with him to Paris the addresses of various contacts you might need in emergencies."

After discussing a few more routine matters we parted, and I returned to the Porchester to arrange for my journey.

All outgoing aircraft to Paris were booked up for the rest of that day, and there was no justification for getting any priority, so I rang up one of our Air Ministry contacts to see if any service machine was on a routine run to anywhere via Paris. I could easily have gone by boat, but I was impatient.

"The only thing we can offer you tonight, Paul," said the friendly booming voice, "is the back seat of a Meteor 7, the new two-seat trainer version, which we've got to ferry to a unit in Germany. You are welcome to that, and Paris is no bother if you want to jump out there."

"I shall probably die of claustrophobia in that thing, Bill, but I willingly accept. Where and when?"

Three hours later I was signing the routine form—the "blood chit"—at Biggin Hill, absolving the Royal Air Force of all responsibility for my person; and a few minutes later was cooped up in the tightest of cockpits, with the two jet engines screaming my head off as they opened up at the end of the runway. After twenty roaring minutes in the air we were landing at Orly airfield near Paris, and I was glad enough to be out of that flying strait-jacket and waving good-bye to the rather melancholy little pilot officer who had charge of the monster.

It had been raining in Paris too and was clearing up as I

drove into the city. When I was comfortably in my room at the Meurice, I opened the window, and as if at my call the sun came out, and the Tuileries Gardens lay stretched out fresh and glistening beneath me. The Tuileries have a special appeal for me, as it was from here that the great Professor Charles set off in the first man-carrying hydrogen balloon on December 1, 1783. The air was good to breathe, and I stood there like an advertisement for health salts, inhaling deeply and pulling my chin back.

Caroline and Anne were in when I rang the George V, and we arranged to meet there at six-thirty for cocktails. Caroline said she was feeling "quite well"—whatever that meant—and when I said we should all be leaving soon for Garda she seemed relieved and glad. I also promised I would report the substance of my interview with Dennis Newcomen.

Next I rang the Langleys, and luckily was through to them in half an hour and was speaking to Nellie.

"Harvey,* my dear, of course we should love to have you, with or without your harem. If you come direct to Verona on the Orient Express and get there on Friday morning I shall meet you, unless you are flying to Milan. Who is this Caroline Norton, by the way? Do I know her? Anne, of course, we both know."

I explained briefly that Caroline was an ex-WAAF officer who was recuperating from an injury, and that I would tell all when I saw her; the "all" being the new half-true story about the Resistance, which would have now to be the rou-

* Ever since the three of us together had seen that delightful play in New York about the invisible rabbit of that name, I had been dubbed "Harvey" by the Langleys. They had always disliked "Paul."

89

tine explanation to be offered to anybody who needed to have an explanation.

I had had enough air travel for the time being, and soon after eight o'clock on Thursday evening we climbed thankfully into the enveloping luxury of a sleeper on the Simplon-Orient Express. I never get tired of that much chronicled train, and the scenic beauty of its course through Europe. I think the three of us felt that we were really off on a holiday. Perhaps it was the illusion of escape, and the prospect of peace and sunlight and beauty. I had described the Villa Campagnola and its owners in detail to the two girls, had told them that the Langleys were two of my closest friends, and that George Langley was an American philosopher and poet who had had the good fortune to possess some money of his own. I added that he had had even better fortune when he met Nellie Dax in Vienna and married her. She was the perfect wife for George, meeting him on his own professional ground in their mutual love of good writing, and balancing his other-worldliness with her robust earthiness and her ability to deal with the world as she found it. She did this with humour, but without cynicism.

I found myself hoping fervently that Caroline would hit it off with Nellie, although it might take time. I watched them in the car with some apprehension when, with Nellie driving, we swept out of Verona in a cloud of dust, and along the road to Peschiera. We had lunched and sight-seen in the city; we had shown Caroline the Pisanello fresco (which she did not like) and the bronze doors of S. Zeno (which she loved), and had bought oranges and melons in the noisy and colourful market.

The road came down to the lakeside at Lazise, and from

90

there onwards I was in one of my special heavens. The sun blazed down from a clear sky, the water lay calm as a pond, and the great encircling mountains came in view ahead of us. Every moment some fresh beauty was revealed—the oleanders, the twisting shoreline, the occasional villas with their white walls and coloured roofs, and above all the cypresses, those trees that should perhaps make one melancholy but never succeed with me. Sometimes they stand by the roadside in tapering ones and twos; sometimes they rise in great clusters; and from time to time they come into view, in an uneven rank, marching stiffly down the mountainside.

"What an exquisite place," said Caroline as we slowed down and stopped to show her one of our favourite views.

"There's the villa, out on that point ahead." Nellie pointed to a distant congregation of trees, with white walls shining through them. "It's right on the lake, and we shall be in perfect time for tea on the terrace. George and Bianca are putting on something special for us." I had never seen Caroline—or for that matter, Anne—look so relaxed and happy.

For the rest of that evening I really believe that none of us thought of Messalina, or the Gestapo, or the war. We were enveloped by the compelling atmosphere of the Villa Campagnola; by its works of art, its books, its restful furniture and decoration, its richly flowering garden, and, above all, its owners. But it was after dinner, when Anne and Caroline had gone to bed, that I felt happiest. In the gathering darkness I sat on the terrace between George and Nellie, and for some time we said nothing, being content to gaze gratefully at the magnificent panorama. The great dark screen of mountains rose before us, with the winking cluster of lights that marked Limone nearly opposite us. To the north the distant lights of Riva and Torbole shimmered over the water. Stretching away from below our feet was the lake itself, with the lazily floating lights—red, white, and yellow —with which the fishermen marked their nets. The warm afternoon breeze—the Ora, as it is called locally—was dying away but still continued gently to ruffle the water.

Nellie took the cigarette holder from her mouth and turned to me. "I like your Caroline, Paul. What is her story? Or rather, what is tellable of her story?"

I told them the standard "Resistance" version of Caroline's history.

"Physical bravery is very enviable," said George, "and bravery of that sort in a woman is extraordinary, and admirable." He stretched out his thin legs and leaned far back in his steamer chair, looking up at the sky. "Also, I suppose one appreciates it even more when the person concerned is so delightful; brave people are not always so personable, I've found."

"Are you in love with her, Harvey?" asked Nellie. "That is a silly question, I know, but I have the feeling you are. But seriously, she is a real dear—and that is high praise from a critical Continental like me, as you know."

"You are accusing me of grossly unethical conduct, my dear, and secretly hoping I am guilty of it." And we laughed it off.

But Nellie had restarted a trend of thought. Just what did I feel about Caroline? I then remembered a passage in George's last book, a passage in which he referred to one of Jung's more admirable doctrines. He spoke of the three principal aspects of woman for man. First, the mother figure; second, the physical woman who is the object of sexual desire; and third, the Anima figure—the woman who wears for man the aspect of the *femme inspiratrice,* who stands for him as "the mistress of his inner psychic life." That last was his own exact phrase. Well, I thought, it nearly fits Caroline, where I am concerned. I have known only one other such woman in my life, but she combined this last of Jung's aspects with the second—to my near destruction. I hoped, for my peace of mind, that Caroline would not invade me with such powerful forces. I believe that the phenomenon we call "falling in love" comes about (for a man) when any two of those aspects are fused—any two. That, I believe, accounts for the very different, sometimes startling, and yet perfectly genuine, types of that enviable incandescence. But my feelings for Caroline were beginning to worry me a little, I confess.

Nellie turned again to look at me. "It must be awfully awkward, Harvey, if a psychiatrist really does fall in love with one of his patients. What does he do about it?"

"Oh," I answered, "he tries to cure himself or else gets the hell out of her life."

I spent four very happy days at the villa, and I think they were happy for all of us. The quiet and almost solemn charm of George Langley had its effect even on Caroline; I think if he had been her psychiatrist he might have succeeded in bringing her out and persuading her deepest disturbances to make the surface. She seemed at complete ease with him, and I found myself alternately envious of his power and sad that he was not trained as a doctor. I could then have relinquished Caroline to him. As a matter of fact, I think their relationship did materially help her. With

93

Nellie she was a little reserved at first, because I think Caroline found it hard to adjust herself quickly enough to Nellie's differences of mood, and her way of changing abruptly from intense sympathy and awareness to an apparently flippant superficial gaiety. But before I left, Caroline seemed to have appreciated that curious oscillation, and accommodated herself to it. I was a little sorry for Anne, whose brain and spirit were formed in different patterns; but she was a robust person. Her spontaneous sympathy had sustained Caroline in the dark days, and it was a solid and reliable sympathy, too. I think she found herself a little out of her depth sometimes. But the Langleys, both of them, seemed able to operate at any level of perception, and Caroline felt spiritually at one with them.

On the fifth morning after our arrival I received the letter I knew must come. George Cayley wrote to say that the Brussels pictures had been located and that I could see them as soon as I liked. I wired back that I would leave for Paris the next afternoon, and asked for James Montgomery to meet me at the Meurice for drinks at six the day after.

I told Caroline I would like to have a short talk with her before I left, and we arranged to go out in the boat after tea. It was a tranquil and delightful scene as we set off from the little jetty beneath the terrace. Caroline, in a simple white frock with a huge cartwheel straw hat shading her face, sat in the back of the boat. I rowed in silence for some minutes.

"Caroline," I said, "we have kept off the subject of Helga till now; but I must discuss her, and you, a little before I go back to Paris. I think it is a fair summary to say that in your present state you feel relieved that you know who it is you fear, but are still deeply convinced—even against your reason

—that she is alive and is a threat to you. And that conviction is painful and at times unbearable."

She sat quietly, with her head turned, looking far off at the mountains. We floated in silence under the afternoon sun; a motor horn came faintly echoing over the water, and small ripples slapped gently at the side of the boat.

At last she answered, "I have done my best to sort it out, Dr. Harvard, and I think what you say is fair enough. At present the peace of this place, and the people here, give me security; but I know it can't last, and I also know I must face it. I realize that the fear is quite irrational, even if Helga is still alive; for there is no reason to think she knows or cares about me; unless, of course, she believes I might expose her. But she is very small fry amongst war criminals, I imagine. In London, when I saw her—or thought I saw her—in Bond Street, I don't believe, logically, she could possibly have recognized me, although I cannot help fearing it. I have nearly got to the hopeless state of feeling that I shall have to go on living with this fear until I die, unless I can transcend it." She had lowered her head, and the great brim of the hat hid her face altogether.

"Caroline, before I say anything about your fears, I want to ask you one of those questions you so dislike answering. It is this: Why, when you know you are in the grip of irrational fears, when you have such honesty of purpose and such integrity, why will you not trust me with your thoughts and feelings, no matter how intimate, in the hope that I might help to rid you of those fears? Or, having refused to cooperate except when you are in a really bad phase, why do you not refuse to have anything to do with me and tell Sir George that you want to be out of my care?"

She did not move or utter a word. I waited a minute or so. Never in my career have I so fervently wished, perhaps even prayed, that I might think of the absolutely right words, the immediately appropriate sentence, with which I could help a patient of mine to help herself. The right words would not come. I was conscious of resorting to more dangerous means.

"Is your lack of trust in me due perhaps more to a conviction of my unworthiness for the task? Do you feel that I have not that 'great restfulness, and a full whole and clean disposition, as well in body as in soul'? Or have you been warned that 'those who would become holy speak little of themselves and their own affairs'?"

As I was speaking she raised her head and looked me straight in the eyes. But her face held a curious expression; it was a mingling of surprise and wariness, with more than a trace of anger.

"Dr. Harvard," she started, but her voice was almost faltering, "where did you get those words and why are you saying them to me now?"

"You know perfectly well who wrote them—the anonymous author of *The Cloud of Unknowing* wrote the first, and St. Francis de Sales the second. But before I tell you why I said them I would ask you to note your own expression, and how it supports my belief. 'Where did you *get* those words?' you said, just as if I were a vandal pillaging the altar of God."

I think it was the purely fortuitous circumstance of our being in a boat that prevented Caroline Norton from immediately getting up and leaving, with a vow never to see me again. I could not now catalogue the emotions that possessed her, except that anger seemed to predominate. I went on. "For some reason I cannot yet guess, Caroline, you have always harboured just below the surface of your mind a stubborn pride and a curious contempt for me. Yet another part of you, despised by the other you, has found a use for me, and even feels gratitude towards me—no, no, please don't interrupt for the moment. You are beset by two conflicts: the conflict of your fear of Helga, and the conflict of your feelings for me. The first you cannot face unaided, which is a terrible blow to your pride; the second you *won't* face, as you don't want to see what it is all about.

"Now about why I quoted those two great men. I have realized, or thought I've realized, ever since you left a certain book in my car, that you were studying mysticism. I expect you have been studying it ever since the war, ever since you were aware of subterranean conflicts and unease in your life after the terrible experiences you went through during that period. Possibly you also suffered from an inner feeling of guilt. You probably saw mysticism as an answer, or an escape, or an atonement. Then the conflict was suddenly focused within you, and you could no longer cope; and you were sent to me—inwardly and perhaps half-consciously angry that you had to abandon your own solutions and rely on an ordinary human being for help, and naturally resenting the situation. But some part of you at least recognized my good intentions and proceeded to provide another conflict within you. I believe, Caroline, pride is your only sin, to put it theologically; and pride is one of your two main problems, to put it medically—Helga being the other. At the moment you are terribly angry with me, I know—"

She could no longer hold back her words. For the first

and last time in our acquaintance she really attacked me. Her eyes were blazing, and her whole body was quivering. I noticed abstractedly that, as a result, the brim of her hat was also gently vibrating.

"And what, Dr. Harvard, do you presume to know about religion, and, of all things, mysticism? You, who are the most crudely materialistic person I have ever known, and who only see human beings in terms of body and mind—or rather sex and mind most of the time. I wish I had never gone to Sir George that day, and that—" She suddenly stopped.

"And that you had never set eyes on me," I added. And with that she burst into tears. There was no turning away, no effort to restrain herself. She cried unashamedly. It was then that I heard loud laughter and the thudding of engines coming over the water, and turned to find an excursion steamer fast approaching behind me and to my right. I pulled on one oar until our boat swung round, and then I rowed steadily away from its path, keeping Caroline's back towards it until we were well out of eye range.

"Caroline, do you know this is the first time you have allowed yourself to behave like a human being in front of me, except just at first when you were very ill?" I pushed my clean handkerchief between her fingers. "Now please listen. You may not believe it, but I am quite well read in the subject of mysticism. What is more, I believe it is the highest form of experience available to the human being. If you are capable of its disciplines and its mode of direct intuitive experience, you will follow the teaching until you achieve what Eckhart calls 'the identity out of the One into the One and with the One.' But if you try to use it as an

98

escape, you will never succeed. It is for the strong, not the weak. If, after you have got over your psychological fears, you turn to it for its own sake, then you will triumph and nothing can stop you. Your fears are on a low level of being; they have to be cured on a low level—on my sort of level, if you like. Once done, you would, quite rightly, have no more use for me. Then you would be free to go your own way, in whatever direction suited you. What you have been trying to do—please believe me—is to use mysticism as a means to an end. You cannot succeed in that, for the simple reason that it is an end in itself."

She had now dried her tears and was looking, as she had earlier, far away towards the mountains. She was not angry any more, or so I felt.

We said nothing until we came within sight of the villa, when Caroline looked at me with a puzzled but almost friendly expression, and said, "Dr. Harvard, why did you read a lot on that subject and now virtually disclaim any achievement in it?"

I thought it would do no harm to tell her the truth, so I said, "Fifteen years ago I asked a very lovely and wonderful person to marry me, and she refused. It took years of pain, a lot of reading, and much thought to resolve my feelings. I also had to know the road she had taken, although I could never follow her. You see, Caroline, I had fallen in love with a saint; and for an ordinary person like me that meant an almost unbearable situation."

She again turned her head away. "I am sorry for what I said to you just now," she almost whispered, as if talking to herself.

99

8

I left Lake Garda the next day, and Nellie drove me into Verona to catch the Orient Express. It reached Paris the day after; and, with my few days of escape already a nostalgic memory, I waited for James Montgomery in the lounge of the Hotel Meurice. He arrived punctually at six, and we had a few drinks at the bar. We talked trivialities—mostly about birds—and then took a taxi to the Bois, where we could talk in peace and without being overheard.

James Montgomery was a formidable young man, and I could not have asked for a better assistant. He had had a legal training, was trilingual—in English, German, and French, with a fair command of Italian and Spanish—had been a good half-miler and swimmer at Cambridge, had been put through a variety of tough and informative courses by George Cayley and his colleagues, and in addition had been sent to take an F.B.I. course in Washington.

In appearance he was of average height, dark, and with a melancholy expression communicated chiefly through his sad brown eyes. But he was far from melancholy, and indeed I thought his present assignment would prove rather tedious for such an active person. But I much enjoyed his company, especially as his hobby was bird-watching. Like most bird-lovers, he was oddly ignorant of, and uninterested in, how birds flew. As this was the only aspect of their life I understood, I felt I could retain a little conversational dignity when I was not listening, fascinated, to his experiences on obscure Scottish islands observing the sea birds.

On George Cayley's advice I kept Caroline Norton completely out of the account I gave James Montgomery. The fewer people who knew about her the better. So I went carefully over the whole Monkey case and the Messalina case. I naturally gave him a description of who and what Helga Bamberg was, and told him she was wanted by George Cayley on a number of counts, including the torturing of some of his agents. The finding of Monkey himself, or the definite proof of his death, I put to James as of equal importance with the tracing of Messalina.

The first thing we decided upon was the systematic watching of the Galerie Houdon. Every person bringing or removing a picture was to be shadowed in the hope of getting some lead on Jean Redel or the purchasers of his works. This surveillance might at first waste a lot of time and involve a considerable number of men, but James had been given the necessary facilities for laying on these observers, and I left that part of the business entirely to him. I would not even know the watchers by sight, and would only take over once they had a lead. But all the men knew me well by sight and would get in touch with me as soon as was necessary, using a different password each day.

James suggested the admirable safety measure of photographing every one of the "carrying" visitors to Monsieur Joubert's establishment, as well as anyone who might remotely be taken for Redel. This would be done with those ingenious little cameras that to a casual passer-by look like fat fountain pens, which are fitted with a wide-angle lens and a roll of microfilm giving twenty exposures. James was also to explore the possibility of gaining access to Joubert's account books; but we had little hope of success in that.

James stayed in Paris to get all this organized. I left on the midnight train for Brussels and next morning paid a visit to the British Embassy, where I was to be looked after and piloted to a depository on the outskirts of the city. It was here that the Monkey pictures had been located, with the somewhat surprised cooperation of the Belgian government officials. The counsellor told me that he would turn me over to a young press attaché named Osborne who knew Brussels well.

My temporary assistant proved friendly, humorous, and, happily, a complete extrovert. We set off in an embassy car amid a downpour of rain, and after nearly half an hour—much of it spent bumping over cobbled streets—we drew up beside the huge gaunt building to which our paintings had been traced.

We were expected, and after we had spent a minute or two in a dirty, paper-strewn office presided over by a surprisingly smart young woman in black, an enormous Belgian arrived to announce that he was the assistant manager and completely at our service. We followed him up three flights of stairs and through a long barnlike room loaded with furniture and boxes, and finally out over an open bridge connecting with a second building. At last we entered another long storeroom lit entirely by large skylights, and apparently filled with furniture draped in white covers. But at the far end we could see a section of tall wooden racking filled with pictures, their gilt frames leaning against one another like giant volumes in a bookcase.

Our guide was panting a little and holding his fine stomach with both hands by the time he came to a halt in front of the racks.

"Here are the pictures, Messieurs. I had them dusted off yesterday. I hope they are what you want." He began to pull one out, and nearly dropped it. "The most extraordinary pictures I ever saw," he added, looking at it, "but everyone to his taste."

"They are unpleasant objects," I answered, "but I am a crime psychologist and have to study such things."

"Ah," said the fat Belgian, "that is interesting." He held the picture at arm's length. "Poor woman. Well, Messieurs, I will leave you to come down when you are ready. You will be able to find your way?" We said yes. *"Bon,"* he said, put down the picture, and rolled away down the avenue of draped furniture.

"For heaven's sake, what on earth are these things?" asked Osborne.

I turned to find Osborne staring down at the picture the Belgian had taken from the rack. It showed a severed woman's head—painted life-size—thrust forward for exhibition by the great bony hand of the executioner, which grasped it by the hair. The face was, without doubt, the face of our Messalina.

"Yes, they will all be somewhat like that," I said. "Do you mind helping me, or would you prefer to wait downstairs? I shall be rather a long time, I'm afraid."

"Oh, it's all right with me, sir; my instructions were to help you all I could, and if it's only looking at some grim pictures, I can take it all right. What do you want me to do?"

103

As he was speaking I had been unloading the gear from my case—a Leica with a battery flashbulb attachment, which I gave Osborne to put together; two magnifying glasses; two torches; a note pad; a measuring tape; and a box of large adhesive red labels. Then we got down to work. There were thirty-two paintings, and the first thing to do was to separate those in which Messalina figured and fix a red label to each one in case they had to be sent for later. These numbered about half the total, there being some doubtful ones in which the face or faces were obscured. But two remarkable facts struck me at the first quick search. First of all, two of these pictures were clearly very much like those handled by the Galerie Houdon—at least, the Marquise de Brinvilliers picture was definitely similar; and from Joubert's description the La Spara seemed almost certainly to be in the same category. If two were similar, how many more? And what did this repetition mean? I decided to come back to these problems when we had catalogued the whole lot. The second point was that the amount of nudity in the paintings was less before Messalina appeared on the scene. Afterwards Monkey took every opportunity to unclothe Messalina and the other victims he included.

I dictated a description and notes on each painting, including dimensions, which Osborne took down. Next we photographed each canvas and, where a clear Messalina face appeared, made an extra close-up of it. In addition, with a special lens, I took nearer close-ups of individual Messalina features such as ears, eyes, and mouths. While this laborious routine was in progress my companion was laudably silent, and only occasionally made grunts of disgust or surprise—

one didn't know which was which. Only when we had finished, and before I began a proper examination of the more important works, did he lean back, stretch, and deliver himself on the subject of Messalina with admirable restraint. "Those women certainly got it in the neck, didn't they?"

From the pictures in which she featured, I chose for careful study, first of all, the Brinvilliers and the Spara; next the large severed head; and then half a dozen more which showed Messalina's features most clearly. I told Osborne that I should not need his help for the rest of the time, so he said he would go down and exercise his legs, and then sit in the car until I was ready.

I was left alone with my gallery of torment, and set about examining the selected pictures. With one of the magnifying glasses fitted with a small electric light I went over every inch of canvas, watching how Monkey had laid on his paint, how he handled his lights and shadows, and his colour. Particular attention had to be paid to the eyes, ears, and mouth of each face, as these parts tend to follow a habitual pattern of brushwork and handling with most artists.

Then I stood back and absorbed as much as I could of the mood and general character of each painting. Monkey must be—or have been—a curious and pathetic character, for all his fortitude and usefulness to the Service. For these pictures were painted with an almost overpowering emotional absorption. There was a tone of satisfying sexual revenge about them, as if the artist were settling accounts with the whole female sex—or rather the matriarchal members of the sex, as summed up in the face and figure of Messalina. Her arrival seemed to have focused his feelings. It was as if he were immunizing, through these images, a collective and dangerous woman of a very definite type. I wondered what his mother had been like.

Before I left Brussels I wrote a full report for George Cayley, and next morning, on my way to the station, dropped it at the embassy for inclusion in their London bag. Once back in Paris, I left a note for James Montgomery to meet me that evening, and then went to the Louvre to clear my head and impose some harmony on my spirit. As I sat in front of Angelico's "Annunciation" my whole attitude and feelings came quickly under its spell of serenity, and after half an hour I left the building without looking at anything else, well satisfied with my state of mind.

James and I sat over our cocktails in a corner of Fouquet's, and I gave him a careful account of the Brussels pictures and of my speculations about Monkey, and handed my films over to him for developing. I was now more than ever anxious to study some of the Redel pictures to see if they were by the same hand. The nocturnal examination of Brinvilliers was too distant to appraise brushwork, although one could sense the mood of the picture fairly well. We planned to press Alexis Joubert for his promised photograph of the Spara painting, and I decided to visit him in the near future.

But the real problem was to obtain access to a considerable number of Redel's paintings, and it was to that task we bent our brains. The obvious route was via Joubert's account books. The matter was so important that I decided to return to London and ask Cayley how far we could go—or rather how far the Service could go in helping us. Of equal importance was the identification and location of Redel himself, although we realized that if he suspected anyone was

106

on his trail he would probably disappear. In fact, even when we had tracked him, as I was sure we should, our mere appearance in his studio would probably cause him to bolt immediately afterwards, because he must know that under ordinary circumstances nobody would be able, or want, to find him.

It turned out to be fortunate that I flew over to London, as George Cayley had another and urgent job for me—a routine examination of one of his agents—so it was two days before I could have a long quiet talk with him about the Messalina case. He took the afternoon off, and we had Alfred drive us to Marlow for tea. All the way there, and during tea, and all the way back, we discussed the case and especially the two essential tasks ahead—to find Redel, and to see his pictures. Cayley agreed that the account book would have to be looked at to locate the pictures, but it was not likely to have Redel's address in it. We finally agreed that a minor criminal action would have to be carried out. In England a number of excuses and methods could be found for discreet entry into business premises, but to do it in France without official cognizance was a totally different matter. We had, of course, discussed the wisdom of enlisting the help of the French police on some fabricated story, but Cayley decided we might need their help later on, and it was better not to seek it too early in the game. So crime it would have to be, although we could not help feeling it was both mean and sordid, despite the necessity.

9

Our raid on the Galerie Houdon was carefully planned and executed. James first cased the shop very thoroughly, and we got to know that Joubert's woman assistant generally left a good hour before he did. So we set the time for a Friday, and, on the evening before, I wrote a letter to Joubert saying I was going to call during the afternoon of the next day to see if he had any news of the Redel photograph he had promised me. At a few minutes before six James entered the Galerie Houdon. He was rather loudly dressed, skilfully made up to look some twenty years older than his age, and spoke with an American Midwestern accent. I had been following at about twenty yards. By looking in various windows near by I gave him five minutes and then entered the shop. If there had been another customer inside, James would simply have been asking Joubert about a picture and I would have waited until he had left. If all was well, and it was, James was to have looked round the shop and led Joubert to the rear of the establishment to discuss the purchase of a nude at the end of what he had nicknamed "Easel Alley." One could easily imagine the sequence of events. One last look round; then James's hand pointing; Joubert's head turned to look; then a quick but not too severe blow with a small rubber cosh.

When I opened the street door I saw at once that there

had been no hitch. I twisted the catch on the lock and so locked the door from the inside, walked silently down the thick carpet between the easels, and bent over the unfortunate Joubert, who had brought down a picture of Old Paris in his fall and now lay motionless on the floor in a black pin-striped heap. We were well out of the line of vision from the street, where the only viewing point at head height was through the glass door. I bent down, pulled up Joubert's left sleeve, undid his cuff, and pushed up his shirt sleeve. The hypodermic was ready in my pocket with a sterilized cover over the needle. It was the work of some fifteen seconds, on our rehearsal timing, to dab his arm with a wad of cotton wool soaked in ether and pump a light dose of pentothal into a vein of his arm. That would keep him out for about twenty minutes.

I called out the agreed word, "Raffle," and James put out the shop lights, which one of our men had prospected beforehand at the price of a small corner of Old Paris. (I wondered at the time how that purchase would figure in the accounts we would later send to Cayley.) I next put on some thin cotton gloves, pulled out my torch, and by its light removed Joubert's pocketbook, which I dropped on the carpet after taking out the money. By the time I had readjusted the victim's shirt and coat sleeve I was already aware of muttered profanity coming from James in the near-by office. I gave him a quarter of an hour, during which time he should have been copying from the account book, or microfilming it if he was doubtful about the correct names. I called out softly to him and told him the time was up. He immediately appeared in the doorway and, owing to the possibility of Joubert's coming slowly round and remembering us talking, he walked straight by me and out of the shop, only muttering, "No luck," as he passed. I wondered what he meant by that, but was too busy to bother, as there was work to be done. I put on the lights and went out into the street. There was no policeman in sight, so I asked a passer-by to tell the first *agent* he saw that I had discovered a wounded man in the shop and would stay with him until help arrived.

I had not long to wait. Joubert was just coming to, and I was holding his head solicitously, when a small and dapper policeman arrived and, with a justifiably suspicious look at me, asked what had happened.

"I do not know, Monsieur, but from this empty wallet and the bruise on this man's head, I imagine he has been attacked and robbed. I am a doctor, and luckily it does not seem to be serious. I came to see Monsieur Joubert here, and found him lying stretched on the floor. I thought something was wrong when I pushed open the door, as the lights were not on; it is dark in here even on a bright day. After examining him, I stayed with him for some minutes before asking the first person I saw to fetch the police. I wondered whether to try telephoning, but I am not very familiar with your police calls."

"You did quite correctly, Monsieur. We must wait till he recovers."

By now Joubert was coming up through the pentothal quite gently and slowly. I went to find some water, and when I returned the policeman was trying to question Joubert and had obviously been asking him if it was I who had attacked him. But the patient, just as obviously, was as yet too vague to know what it was all about.

Finally he came properly to his senses and looked at both of his rescuers with surprise. The policeman then asked him straight out if I was his attacker—I admired him for that—and poor Alexis Joubert wagged his head.

"No, no, Monsieur, it was a *sacré* American—a man in a loud suit, about fifty, who pretended he wanted to buy a picture and led me here to the back of the shop before attacking me. This is Dr. Harvard, who is well known to me and whom I was expecting this afternoon."

"Superintendent Claudel, of the Police Judiciaire, will vouch for me," I said. "I am quite well known to him and some of his colleagues."

The little policeman nodded his head and vigorously wrote all this down in a notebook before going to the telephone and ringing his station. He now looked at me kindly in my newly established role of succourer.

While we were waiting for more police Alexis Joubert thanked me profusely. I asked how much he had had in his wallet. On being told it was twenty thousand francs I persuaded him to accept the amount from me as a loan, or on account of future purchases—in different notes from those I had taken, needless to add. I am glad to say he made little fuss about this and was grateful without being effusive. The policeman was much impressed by this token of my innocence and was about to make some appropriate remark when his colleagues arrived and we went through the whole story again. Although Joubert's head was hurting him considerably, and I told him he must go to bed, he insisted on going to the Quai des Orfèvres straight away to see if he could recognize his assailant in the rogues' gallery at headquarters. I went along too, so that I could make a signed statement and have my acquaintance with Claudel checked. But when we arrived Joubert was not feeling too well, and I made him lie down. It was not until three hours later, after he had sufficiently recovered to examine the photographs, that I took him home in a taxi. As we neared our destination we spoke for the first time about our business.

"I will come round to the shop again soon," I said. "I only wanted to know if you had secured the photograph of Redel's painting you kindly said you might get for me; or to know if you could show me some of the descriptions of the pictures, with, of course, your clients' names and the prices covered over." We both laughed.

"Alas, Monsieur, both requests would have been impossible to satisfy today," he answered. "The photograph is at this very time being printed for you and will soon be ready; and as for the descriptions, they are, as I told you, in my ledger. But last night I took it home with me to check, and by some extraordinary lapse of memory I forgot to bring it back to the Galerie today."

10

It was a very annoyed pair of Englishmen who strolled in the Bois next morning.

"Well, it can't be helped," I said. "It was just impossibly bad luck, and that's that. But we certainly cannot try it again. For the time being we must focus our hopes on our observers and try to track either Redel or the buyers. It will obviously be some time before another picture is completed and called for—unless, of course, Redel has an accumulated stock and decides to part with another one fairly soon. But we must keep everyone on the alert, even if they have to sweat it out for weeks."

I could not help feeling sorry for Alexis Joubert, but James had no sympathy for him. "After all," he said, "I scarcely tapped him, and I shouldn't be surprised if he isn't mixed up with some other dirty business apart from this picture racket."

"What makes you think that?" I asked. The same thought had occurred to me, but I had no reason to believe he was playing outside the law, and I had put it down to my general dislike of the man.

"Well, for one thing, there is a very peculiar safe in his office, a most unusually modern one with all sorts of electrical trips and gadgets, I should imagine, by the look of it. Why does a picture dealer, as such, have that sort of safe?

Certainly not to keep his ledgers in. After all, supposing we—or anyone else for that matter—did get a look at the book; it would only lead at worst to spoiling a small part of his market or upsetting his clients. No, that safe means something very different, unless I am woefully mistaken."

This was something quite new on our horizon. For some minutes we ranged over the lines of business Joubert might be in, from espionage, via drugs, to receiving stolen goods. If the latter, it was probably jewellery, as James said that the safe was a small one. But drugs would also be possible. However, apart from reporting this to Cayley, we would have to keep strictly to our own business.

By the time we left the Bois we could count on no new ideas and were grudgingly resigned to the watch-and-wait technique of our observers. And yet I felt there must be some way to force the issue—the apparently simple issue of tracking down a few pictures. But with no leads, and both secretive sellers and secretive buyers, the task was far from easy in a foreign country.

As we settled back in our taxi I began to feel more and more stubborn. "I'm damned if I'll lie down and wait for those miserable old spiders to crawl out of their holes," I said.

"I know, Doctor. I was wondering if we could advertise in the papers and say that a reward would be offered to anyone giving information about pictures by Redel. But I'm afraid that would immediately tip off the artist himself; and in any case the buyers don't seem in need of money. We cannot bribe them that way."

That one word "bribe" suddenly shone out in my mind like a beacon.

"Bribe," I said. "We may not be able to bribe them with money; but what about bribing them with other pictures of the same subjects? We could easily commission such pictures ourselves."

"But how would we get the news over to them that a new supply was opening up, without again making either Joubert or Redel suspicious?" he asked.

"Yes, that is always what we come up against—this wretched question of avoiding attention and yet getting what we want and getting it fairly soon. But—wait a minute, something else is coming to me."

At that moment the taxi drew up at the Meurice, and we got out. We went straight to the bar and settled ourselves in a corner.

James Montgomery looked almost excited as we waited for our drinks to be set down and watched the waiter out of earshot. "Well?" he said. "What is the idea?"

"We have, I think, been going about our thinking in too stereotyped a way. Why don't we work through Joubert to his clients? Surely he could be forced to get us a sight of his clients' pictures if we could make it worth his while. And the way to make it worth while is by offering him something those clients of his will want."

"Yes, but what could we offer? Joubert himself could probably commission more paintings of the right kind to increase the supply if he wanted to, couldn't he?"

"That worries me too; but there may be various explanations for why he does not. First of all, he might well find it difficult to persuade a competent enough artist to do such subjects. Most of the respectable and able academic painters would probably be horrified by the idea; such activity would soon come out and possibly ruin their orthodox careers. Secondly, Joubert might not even have thought of it. He may be quite content to carry on quietly, especially if he is involved with something else that is equally lucrative and really criminal. But he might be well enough pleased to sell new material provided he was not involved in commissioning it himself. Therefore there is a chance—the more I think of it, a very good chance—of tempting him by offering him good meat for his clients with no trouble for himself—including, of course, a fair rake-off into the bargain. Therefore, what can we offer him?"

We discussed this new approach. I was fairly confident of being able to get an English artist to do some vividly unpleasant pictures, but they would be no better than Redel's, and it might even be difficult to hire someone quite as good. Then there was the time element. We couldn't be at this business forever.

"Now, Doctor, you've given *me* an idea—good heavens!" He sat bolt upright in his chair. "Why on earth don't we get those pictures from the Belgians and offer *them* to Joubert? That would be the finest bargaining material in the world!"

The idea lit up our horizon brilliantly like a star-shell, but only for a moment. I think James saw the snag at the same time.

"No use, James. The moment we offer Joubert one of those pictures he will fairly bristle with suspicion and immediately tell Redel. After all, they will look so like Redel's—even if they are not indeed by him—that the cat will be out of the bag before we even know what kind of cat it is. We would run the risk of Redel's—and Joubert's for that matter—bolting, especially if they realized we had the power to produce the things. It would make us objects of extreme suspicion, and our cover of genuine medical interest would go up in smoke."

James slumped back in his chair and nodded despondently. But out of his disappointment was to come, indirectly, the solution. For after we had been sitting for a minute or two in silence, relaxed in a gloomy fashion—and as we looked round the room aimlessly—James's eye came to rest on a paunchy little man who had a peculiar air of respectability combined with a somewhat shifty appearance.

"That's the sort of man I imagine Joubert's clients to be," said James with a note of irritation in his voice. Then: "Doctor, what is it exactly that these old boys—if they are old—want in these pictures?"

"Ah," I said, "that is a good point. And a good pointer too, because I now realize something I should have realized before. If these pictures fulfil some fantasy needs, then the more actual the picture—that is to say, the more realistic—then the more it will appeal. Therefore if we could find—" Then another idea came to me as if out of the tobacco-laden air of the bar.

"James, have you ever been in the Chamber of Horrors at Madame Tussaud's?" He nodded.

"Well, do you remember they have a long case against the wall with medieval tortures shown in small-scale dioramas —fully modelled figures against perspective backgrounds? I know someone connected with Tussaud's who would put us on to the artist. That would certainly be something we might trade through Joubert, don't you think?"

James leaned back and blew a slow stream of smoke from his mouth. "I am not sure, Doctor. Chiefly there is the time element. I should imagine it would take quite a time to do even a small diorama, wouldn't it?"

I reluctantly agreed, but it was now James's turn to look inspired, and what he suggested finally proved the answer. "It's so obvious that we should be ashamed of ourselves. Photographs—posed photographs of models acting out similar scenes to Redel's. We could produce a whole flock of them in about a week. With expert faking, there's not one of those subjects that could not be reproduced with ten times the grim actuality of our friend Redel. They could be coloured if necessary. And what's more, I think the Service photographic outfit would turn out the stuff for us. What do you think?"

I knew he was right. "Yes, you've got it, I'm sure. It is an excellent idea. And I can go to Joubert and tell him in advance that I should like him to consider an exchange and see how he reacts. We will work out a series of subjects and poses tonight, and you can go over to London tomorrow, tell Sir George, and get busy with our photograph people."

We felt much more hopeful as we went in to lunch—a simple idea had transformed the depression of our morning walk into a confident elation. At two o'clock I set out for the Galerie Houdon, and when I arrived I found Joubert in high good humour, ushering out of his shop a fat and over-made-up woman who—he told me—had bought no less than three corners of Old Paris and the Napoleon, all for her house in Newcastle. "Ah, Monsieur, she has a great love of Paris and of the French!"

I asked him how his head was, heard it was as good as new, and then said I would like a private word with him. We retired to the office, and I was amused to see that the picture that covered the wall safe was slightly ajar and rather incongruous in its doorlike posture. We sat down and lighted cigarettes.

"Monsieur Joubert, I have an idea that might appeal to you. You know already that I am anxious to see as many of Redel's pictures as possible, but I quite understand how you are placed and that it is impossible to put me in touch with the owners or the artist. Now I'm not really concerned with the artist because my patient in London—he is a very rich man, by the way—has a mind very similar to your clients', I should imagine. He has come to me, not because of his peculiar obsession with this subject of punishment, but because he is an alcoholic and is now getting frightened by the hold of drink on him. However, he soon told me about his morbid interests, and I am learning a lot about his mind from studying them. I particularly want to get his reactions to such pictures as Redel paints, even if only in photographs. If he was likely to be able to see the originals, all the better. I tell you this, Monsieur, to give you the background to my proposition. Now, his particular way of satisfying his interests might well form a basis of exchange—through you, of course—with your clients."

Joubert leaned towards me, and he was obviously interested. "A basis of exchange, Monsieur?" he asked. "I do not quite understand."

"Simply this. He has no access to such paintings as you can supply, but, being a rich man, he has commissioned a photographic studio to hire and photograph suitable models who act out these scenes of violence. By means of clever faking and the addition of colour, he has had produced the most vivid and terrible pictures you can imagine."

"And how many of these scenes has he got?" inquired Joubert, showing, I fancied, more interest than he intended.

"Oh, I suppose at least fifty or so; and he owns the negatives, so that they cannot be reproduced without his knowing. So what I propose, if he agrees, is that you offer some of these photographs to your clients and tell them quite openly what the conditions are for their purchase."

"And what would those conditions be, Monsieur?" There was no doubt now that he was interested.

"That, for each photograph purchased, one of Redel's paintings is brought here—at my expense—and taken to your gallery upstairs, where my patient and I can see it and it can be photographed for me to study later. In that way I shall never know who owns them or where they have come from. In practice, what I suggest is that you tell me how many Redel pictures you have disposed of to your clients, and I will bring a selection of photographs for them to choose from, with a stock of extra ones for you to dispose of to them in the future. Then they can have the photographs in bulk, so to speak—paying whatever you wish to charge them, of course—and send their pictures here all together. That will save my patient and me a lot of time. Now, Monsieur Joubert, what do you think of my offer? I want to emphasize that I have no interest whatever in the identity of your clients."

Joubert lay back in his chair and made a steeple out of his thin white hands. He examined the ceiling with great care. Then he jerked his head forward.

"I think I can arrange it, Monsieur. I think your offer is a fair one. I confess that at first I thought you were also interested in my clients. But now I think you are being frank with me. I shall have to have the photographs for a few days so that I can show a few examples to my clients—to see their reactions. If they are favourable, I shall ask them to send all their pictures to me and then allow them to call here and take away an equal number of your photographs when the pictures are safely upstairs. Is that agreeable to you, Monsieur?"

I said it suited me perfectly, and he also agreed to have a photographer he could trust on hand to take photographs of the Redel pictures according to my instructions. I had an idea that he was not intending to inform the clients that their pictures would be photographed while on temporary loan to the Galerie Houdon.

We fixed a day three weeks ahead for my visit to bring him the photographs, and I secretly hoped that period would be sufficient for James Montgomery to have our "firm" produce them.

"By the way, Monsieur Joubert," I asked as we got up, "how many pictures, approximately, will you have for me to see, provided your clients agree to our arrangement? I shall then know approximately how many photographs to bring."

He looked up at the ceiling again and counted quietly to himself. "I should say about thirty, Monsieur."

I thanked him, and we were about to shake hands when he remembered the photograph he had promised me. He turned over some papers on his desk and pulled forth a large brown envelope. He took out the photograph, and one could see at once that it was not an exact duplicate of the Brussels picture but a very similar variation, as if the artist had been painting a subject he had done before and was working from his memory of it. However, we should soon have the evidence of the originals. Thanking Joubert again, I put the print back in its envelope, tucked the thing under my arm, and made my departure.

That evening, in the lounge of my hotel, James and I sat with paper and pens, intent on the macabre occupation of inventing scenes of punishment and slaughter which would satisfy the most morbid of tastes. We recognized that the standard of competition with Redel was high, and that our products must be effective rivals.

"I certainly don't envy you the job of fixing up those arrangements, James."

"Oh, that's easy; but you've got to be there to select the models and supervise the posing—I shouldn't know what was effectively sadistic or not." In my relief at finding a solution to our problem I had completely overlooked this part of the business, and the more I thought of it the less I liked the idea of either of us taking part in the stage work, so to speak. The less we appeared to people outside our work, especially involving such unpleasant items, the better. I said as much to James, and he agreed. But how, then, were we to get exactly what we wanted?

"Well, the photo people keep a very good cover going as a straight commercial photographic firm. They find it useful to keep a lot of contacts in the trade, and they have, I am sure, their contacts with the model agencies as well. Small-time actors and professional models would be hired for this kind of job, I imagine, and a story concocted about doing preliminary stills for a possible horror film."

"I think it will be all right," I said. "We can have ourselves made up by Stanton at Scotland Yard while we are 'on the set,' and with wigs and theatrical make-up we should never be recognized again. It is Stanton who will have to make up my imaginary patient when I take him to Joubert's. I must ask Sir George to give me someone especially for that job. We had better both go back tomorrow and get busy."

James had developed and printed all the Brussels pictures during the afternoon, and he handed me a large envelope full of prints before he left. But I simply could not look at any more violence for the present, so I sealed them up and had the manager put them in the hotel safe. Then I telephoned to my friend Professor Vitel and was delighted to find he had the rest of the evening free. We were always glad to see each other, and we sat up till midnight discussing the work then being done on the study of hypnosis in New York. We were especially interested in the experiments in the much fought-over problem of how far, if at all, a person can be hypnotized and then made to commit a crime of which he would be completely ignorant when awakened from the hypnotic state.

11

Paris was like a furnace when we landed at Bourget from London three weeks later. It was nearly dark, and I wished I could go up in a balloon and stay there in the cool sky until morning, just as the nervy little Madame Blanchard used to do a century ago. I was travelling on a diplomatic passport this time; otherwise I would never have risked transporting our cargo of sordid photographs through the Customs. The thought of what the inspectors would say if they found them was almost amusing, but I was too hot to be amused and too worried to give much thought to tomorrow's mission at the Galerie Houdon.

For I had had a long letter from Anne with the news that Caroline was in another of her bad phases. Before I had read very far, I was afraid it was due to our final talk on Lake Garda, although a fortnight after I left both Anne and George Langley had written to say that she was calm and well. But on reading further it was clear the cause was something else.

It was after a two-day visit to Venice, which all four of them had made, that Caroline had seemed abstracted and worried; that night she told Anne that she had seen Messalina in Chioggia, of all places—the colourful little fishing town on the lagoon a few miles south of Venice. Anne then said that Caroline, although very worried about this new appearance, had calmed down after they returned to the routine of the villa; Anne did not think I need come. I was pleased to hear that Caroline did not react violently as soon as she saw, or thought she saw, the woman.

James Montgomery, along with my pseudo-patient, was to follow in about a week's time. The patient would be wearing slight but skilful make-up, and, having had enough instruction from Stanton to renew it for two or three days, he was to present himself at my room in the Meurice the day after I rang Cayley and reported that all was well.

At ten o'clock next morning I rang Joubert, and he said he would be delighted to see me at any time during the day. So I set off at once, and a quarter of an hour later—with the sad assistant minding the shop—we sat in Joubert's room like two conspirators. The wall-safe painting, I saw with pleasure, was properly in place today. I took out the thick packet of photographic prints, no less than forty-five twenty-by-sixteen-inch enlargements, all of them skilfully hand-tinted. It was some reward for the nightmare existence that James Montgomery and I had been recently leading to see the shocked expression on Joubert's face as he turned over our horrors, one by one. He was by this time, as he said, used to the realism of the paintings, but not to what he was faced with now.

"Monsieur, these things are truly terrible—it is as if they were happening before one's eyes. But of my clients' interest I have no doubt, no doubt whatsoever."

As he continued to gaze at one after another of the photographs, the scenes of the past three weeks were vividly in my mind: scenes of James Montgomery and myself describing—mercifully for us, in George Cayley's presence—our demands to the head of our Service photographic branch, who had borne them with fortitude and disgust; the parade and selection of the female models from the agency, and, to our surprise, the blasé acquiescence with which they heard what was expected of them, as if this were mild compared with what was required elsewhere. Next, the men who would have to act the parts of the executioners—they seemed just as blasé too. Then the assembling of the stage properties, which was quickly arranged through a film company; and finally the posing and photographing of the long series of lurid tableaux.

It was here that James Montgomery had suddenly shown extraordinary initiative and energy. The studio manager and I were amazed by the tricks and fake shots—to avoid retouching as far as possible—whereby he made our sophisticated employees appear headless or dismembered, seem to hang grotesquely from the pasteboard gallows, and otherwise to undergo execution or torture in a score of ways which were staged with unnerving realism—unnerving, that is to say, to all of us but the victims themselves, who seemed after a time even to relish their daily destruction. It was also James who suggested and devised the close-up shots of severed heads and decapitated bodies which proved so successful in their verisimilitude that on one occasion the studio manager and I came briefly to the brink of hysterics. We had been talking to our favourite model, a buxom beauty named Mollie with a ready sense of humour undoubtedly gained in the music halls, who was not taking part in the current tableau. Despite her lively company, we decided to leave her and go out for some stiff whiskies. We returned to the studio an hour later to find James Montgomery, axe in hand, contemplating a scene which sent us hurrying back to the corner tavern. For there was a large naked woman—I recognized Mollie's figure immediately—lying bound and decapitated beside the headsman's block, with blood all over the place—and, as I said, James holding the axe. He told us afterwards that he had painted a red band round the top of Mollie's neck and covered her head with a black sawdust-coated cloth, which was then made to merge with the surrounding props and draperies.

"As a matter of fact, Doctor," he said, "when you two appeared on the scene I had just told Mollie to keep still, and I heard her mumbling through the cloth, 'Where's my bloody head supposed to be, Jimmy?' And that was exactly what I was trying to figure out—where to place her for the second part of the double exposure so that her head could be added."

Joubert finally selected six of the most gruesome shots, including Mollie in the scene described, and told me he would immediately contact his clients. I was to ring again the day after tomorrow, when we could fix a convenient date to see the assembled pictures, provided his clients agreed to the proposition. Both of us had little fear of their refusing.

A message came three days later to say that the offer was accepted, and I rang George Cayley with the news. He seemed pleased and then gave me, in a suitable circumlocutory manner, the latest reports from the team of observers. Nobody carrying a picture to the Galerie Houdon had been seen, and the only people carrying canvases away were bona-fide purchasers. Also no thin man who might be Redel had been seen there.

James Montgomery and my patient duly arrived on the morning of the appointed day. We were to meet at my hotel and set off—not including James, of course—at two-thirty. The patient, whose real name I did not—and still do not—know, but whom we called Newbury, looked very distinguished and very worried. He was most skilfully made up, and for all I know I have seen him scores of times since without recognizing him. We set off for the Galerie Houdon and on arrival were greeted almost effusively by Joubert, who immediately escorted us to the upper floor of his establishment, which I had not seen before. As we mounted the narrow staircase I caught sight of the lugubrious lady assistant eyeing us with an expression of unutterable disgust. I did not blame her, especially after our first sight of Redel's pictures, which were set out round the upper room; for she had obviously seen them and knew our business.

But I had not bargained for the behaviour of my patient. He walked into the room, took one look at the panorama of nudity, violence, and blood, and nearly passed out in my arms. We were ahead of Joubert, I am glad to say, so he did not see the man's agitation. I just had time to whisper to him to close his eyes when pretending to examine the pictures individually. He pulled himself together after a second or two and went the round of the canvases, voicing such comments as we had already rehearsed: "Most interesting," "Very well painted," and similar absurdities.

We were soon joined by the photographer, whose camera and floodlights were already prepared at one end of the room, and I went round with him, arranging the details of what we required—a good all-in photograph of each picture and a number of close-ups, which he noted down in a little red-covered notebook. He was brisk and efficient and treated the whole assignment as if it were a purely routine matter.

After a few minutes of polite conversation Joubert left us. Newbury then went through the motions of examining each picture for the benefit of the photographer, and finally sat on a chair with his back to the man. He remained there with his eyes tight shut, doubtless in acute discomfort. For the next half-hour I examined the pictures carefully, but after only a few minutes I was convinced of one vital fact. They were not by the same hand as those at Brussels. There was therefore both a Leder—Monkey—and a Redel. When the pictures were examined closely, although the general style and handling were similar, there was a noticeable and definite difference in the way the paint was put on. The subject matter showed a lot of variation too, when compared with the Brussels set. Often it was only approximately the same grouping of figures, and the gestures and placing were greatly varied. Later on, with the two full sets of photographs to compare, and my memory of the originals, I would have to make a more careful analysis.

The discovery that there were two artists was momentous enough to dominate my thoughts for the present. However, there were still other points of interest immediately evident: the parallel subject matter, in some ten cases; the fact that Messalina figured in all these Redel pictures; and the odd but distinct feeling that she was painted with more sympathy than in the Brussels batch—even, it might be said, with some flattery. What it adds up to, I thought, is that Leder took a strongly emotional pleasure in annihilating his females, especially Messalina, and the nudity was rendered with a highly charged sexuality. Redel, on the other hand, although presenting just as violent a series of events, lends his nudity a somewhat distant air, and paints his portraits of Messalina as if she were almost a martyr. His nudities are topographically feminine, but emotionally neuter. This could surely be due to only one circumstance—Redel must be sexually inverted.

But there was another idea hanging about in the anterooms of my mind, which I could not lay hands on; some other indefinable feature that was also present collectively in these pictures. With the recent case of the Monkey memories to remind me, I dismissed that ghost of an idea with the certainty that it would materialize out of the unconscious of its own accord.

I thought it might be useful to examine the backs of some of the pictures to note what kind of canvas was used and to see if there were any makers' stamps on them. They were ordinary canvases, but there were no marks. But as I was about to turn the fourth picture round the right way and put it back against the wall, I noticed what looked like some dirty white crystalline powder down between the bottom stretcher and the canvas. Had I not been looking almost vertically downwards I could not have seen it. My first thought was, irrelevantly, of sugar; but almost at once another idea struck me which, although improbable, was worth toying with. Having looked round to make sure the photographer was absorbed with his work, I pulled out my penknife, opened it, licked the blade and pushed it down to where the white substance was lodged. When I withdrew the blade a small amount of the powder was adhering to it; I quickly took out my handkerchief, wrapped it round the knife, and put it in my pocket.

After thanking the photographer in advance for his work, I took the white-faced Newbury downstairs to say good-bye to Joubert. The proprietor was still in a good humour and thanked us for coming. We promised to bring round the bulk of our photographs as soon as he told me the Redel prints were ready to collect. Then we left.

The next thing to be done was to take poor Newbury into the nearest bar and buy him a lot of whisky.

"Good heavens, Harvard, if I had known what I was in for I would have prayed Sir George to excuse me the assignment. How can you stand such things? Or are you so blasé that the sight of naked women being hanged or having their heads cut off leaves you unmoved?"

I wondered where in Cayley's catalogue he was docketed and what his history was. He reminded me of one of my American aunts.

"My dear man, I had no idea you would feel that way. I felt certain that Sir George would have warned you about the nature of the business. As to whether I am unmoved, the answer is yes, rather naturally. Psychiatrists have to look at thousands of drawings and paintings, most of them far worse than those—or rather, more indecent from the ordinary person's point of view. To us they are simply clues—evidence, if you like, as to what is going on in a patient's mind; they are also, of course, boring or interesting according to the rarity or otherwise of the specimens and the symptoms. Just occasionally, if taken unawares, one might have a twinge of surprised unpleasantness left over from one's innocent years"—I was thinking of the decapitated Mollie—"but there is no place in our attitude for disgust or disapproval, or even for dislike. We look upon what you would

131

call perverts as people who are, without knowing it, behaving in a childish or confused way. It is our job to get them right, provided they want to get right and will cooperate. Sometimes, of course, we only abate the nuisance, and sometimes we fail altogether."

"But good gracious, man, what on earth makes a person paint, or look at, such things?"

"Oh, there are many causes and many manifestations; the relevant textbooks will tell you if you are really interested. But to show you roughly how one can approach such things, just consider the general character of those pictures for a minute. There is a lot of nudity—nudity being in essence attractive—and a lot of destruction of that nudity. In the ordinary way you want to destroy what you fear or what threatens you. If then you feel an urge to destroy, or render harmless, what in ordinary circumstances people find attractive, there has obviously been built into your mind a feeling that an attractive female is also a threatening female—a situation which can be brought about, for example, by possessive or dominating mothers, or similar causes. That's the end of the lecture. Have another whisky."

"Well, I suppose I see a little what you mean, but it seems to be a ridiculous and disgusting state to get into."

"My dear Newbury," I said, "one doesn't have to go far with oneself, one's neighbours, or people in general, to meet the ridiculous. As to disgust, look at the origin of the word; it comes from two words which originally meant 'to dislike the taste of.'"

I wondered what he would have said if I had suggested that his extreme reaction to the pictures might be due to a deep-seated fear that any such treatment by him of a female would bring about some terrible retaliation. I packed him off to London next morning with a note for Cayley asking for a conference during the following week.

A few days later I was ready to go. I had arranged to meet James for a last talk after exchanging our photographs for Joubert's. The careful analysis of the pictures must wait for London. James was to stay on in Paris for reports from the observers, while I flew back to London for the conference with Cayley.

As soon as James appeared in the hotel lounge I knew from the curious look of triumph in his eyes that he had important news.

"You must have news," I greeted him, "with an expression like that on your face."

"Yes, Doctor, I have. I think we have traced Redel. One of our men not only followed him—if it is he—back to his home, but believes he has enough photographs for identification. I have got the roll on me now and will give you prints tomorrow to take back to London."

12

We were high over the Channel, and I was dozing in the stuffy atmosphere of the aircraft. A bump caused me to open my eyes lazily, and in a pleasant no-man's-land between dream and reality I contemplated as many of my fellow passengers as I conveniently could without moving my head. My gaze had travelled from the swept-up hair-do of a rather pretty woman who sat ahead of me on the other side of the gangway. It travelled down the back of her seat and then to her right foot, which rested just on the edge of the gangway carpet. On the carpet at that point was a worn patch, and as my eyes settled on that patch a memory stirred and came to me—easily this time—of four rubbed patches. But they were not on a carpet. They were four rubbed patches, each one on a stretcher of a painting—the four pictures I had turned over and examined at Joubert's.

I had not consciously noticed them, but my mind must have automatically absorbed the information for later use. Those patches, coming regularly on four pictures selected by chance, might well mean that export licence stamps had once been there and later erased by someone who did not want them seen. The canvases, I was willing to bet, came into France from another country with pictures already painted on them. That, if true, was highly significant; it made Redel both an agent and a front—but no artist. The photographs James had given me before I left showed a dark, rather sickly man in his thirties. We would get busy on him later. Already there would be a watcher twenty-four hours a day on his flat in the rue de l'Estrapade, near the Panthéon.

I had a busy time that afternoon and evening. First I went straight to Scotland Yard and left the dirty powder for an urgent analysis. Then to the Yard's C.R.O. (the Criminal Records Office) to leave two of the photographs of Redel, one for examination beside their own records in case Redel had crossed their path, and the other to be sent to the International Police Organization at Paris to see if there was anything known of the man there. I told the Inspector that I thought only the name "Redel" should be sent with the photograph to Paris, and not his address.

Then off to my cousin Michael, who is an expert in the technical anatomy of pictures and restoration, to hear what he could tell me about the placing of export licence stamps on modern paintings crossing customs frontiers. His information was that the worn patches on these pictures were just about where such stamps would have been placed. He said that a number of stamps were in use, of similar size, and were put on pictures to guard against the export of national treasures. So we could not guess the frontier, although it was natural to suspect Belgium as the place they came from, pending other evidence.

I had tea with him in his skilfully converted mews house in Knightsbridge, and we talked about our favourite paintings. Then I returned home for an evening to be spent comparing the two sets of photographs. I told Sarah that I did not want her or Alfred to go into the library until tomorrow morning, and then set out the enlargements all round the room until the place looked like a veritable chamber of horrors.

With an hour off for dinner, I worked on those pictures until three in the morning. With strong lights and various kinds of magnifying glasses, I first examined them for brushwork alone, and completely confirmed my belief that we were dealing with two artists. This was also borne out by another, and more psychological, examination of style and general handling, on the lines I had already followed in Paris.

I was interrupted at this point by a call from Scotland Yard to say that the analysis had come through. The powder was heroin. That was what I had thought.

Cayley would certainly be glad that a freak chance had played right into our hands and coincided exactly with his proposed cover story of drug-running. I was thinking of that word "cover," and I suddenly realized why the drug came to be between the canvas and the stretcher of the picture. I picked up the phone, dialled Scotland Yard, and asked for Chief Inspector Yardley. He was off duty, so I gave my name and asked for his deputy, who was there and luckily knew me.

"Have you ever heard," I asked, "of dope-smuggling in the lined canvas of a painting?"

He asked what a "lined" canvas meant.

"If a picture is frail, or has been damaged, you mount it on another canvas. If the painting is modern and the job properly done, you can't detect it from either front or back. I think I have come across a customer who includes a layer of dope between the two canvases."

"No, Dr. Harvard, we've never heard of that method

before, and I'm sure the Chief Inspector will be most interested. I will ask him to contact you on Monday."

I made a mental note to ask Michael how one made a fake lining without removing the stretcher—which must be the case, in view of where I found the powder—and went back to my studies.

The next process was to examine the parallel subject pictures. The more I looked at those "non-identical twins"— the same subjects painted in similar but not identical poses by both artists—the more I felt there was something important I was missing. When the pictures were set side by side I saw that the pairs were indeed not so closely similar as I had thought, especially in poses and grouping. The general arrangement and idea of the pictures were alike. But the faces of the guards and executioners, for example, were completely different, as were the details and colours of their clothes, and also the backgrounds.

By the time I had spent about an hour on these pairs my unconscious processes seemed to be signalling hard, but I could not reach any new conclusion. The situation reminded me of the children's game of Hunt the Thimble, with the onlookers excitedly calling out to the searchers, "Warm; warmer; cooler; warm again; hot; very hot; sizzling"—and then the thimble would be found. I was warm all right, but not yet hot.

On about the fourth survey it struck me that I had not given sufficient attention to the backgrounds and the non-human odds and ends visible in the pictures. So I now concentrated on these. Something told me I was on the right road. I started on a pair showing a Renaissance scene and saw that the buildings visible at the sides of the pictures were very distinct, each one seemingly done with some real building as a model. The Redel building was vaguely familiar to me. Then I noticed the pattern of the stone paving in the Leder; it too was altogether different from its partner and again excited a familiar feeling.

After examining three more pairs, with a mounting sense of imminent discovery, I came to my fifth pair, and there, at last, I found the clue. The pictures in question showed the beheading of a Messalina figure in a medieval setting. The mood of the two pictures was more strikingly different than usual. Leder (Monkey) had staged his scene in a clearly Germanic place with a building like a Gothic Rathaus shown in perspective on the left. Another Gothic building was visible above the heads of the crowd, in the background. In the Redel picture the building seen in perspective was a nondescript Gothic structure. But the building in the background could have existed in only one place, or rather, in one area. It was Venetian Gothic, without any question, with its peculiar but charming window forms as seen, for example, in the Ca d'Oro on the Grand Canal.

I was as excited as a child. I jerked myself out of the chair and made for a tall bookcase by the window. I pulled out Molmenti's *Venice* and began rapidly turning the pages. Once the idea of Venice had been sown in my mind the search became quite easy. For it was the paving pattern in the Renaissance picture that I was after now, and there it was—the paving of the Piazzetta to the west of the Ducal Palace in Venice. Although I had only a few examples to go on as yet, I was now convinced that the Redel pictures were painted in Venice. That city has always been a favourite with me, as it was the first Continental treasure house I saw

138

when a student. I had returned many times since, and its peculiar beauty had remained fresh with me.

As I restudied the picture pairs with Venice in mind, I began to find enough evidence to convince any jury. Pieces of buildings here, a statue there, and sometimes a peculiar but typical ornament, all stood out plainly once I knew what I was looking for. I was wonderfully elated with the success of my art detection, and really felt the Caroline case had at last turned the corner. Like most criminal investigations, the problem had been solved by hard work and close observation.

I decided a slight change of air would do me good, so I left the flat and strolled down as far as Stanhope Gate and then back, trying to keep the whole problem of Messalina and the artists out of my mind. The night was very clear and still, and the park trees looked like stiff stage scenery. I walked back towards Marble Arch and remembered the Z batteries of anti-aircraft rockets that had been there in the war. They had caused much interest when Londoners first saw the strange missiles roaring into the sky.

Then, very faintly, there came to my ears the distant note of a high-flying jet aircraft. It must have been flying at a great altitude, as the noise was only the ghost of a roar. I thought of the pilot up there, secure in his tight little cockpit, with only the faintest glimmer of luminous instruments and the radio crackle in his ears to keep him company. I began to imagine his life—what he had eaten for dinner, what his girl friend was like (or perhaps he was married), and what he was thinking about, all by himself in the vastness of the clear night sky. I once asked a Meteor pilot what he thought about on night manœuvres, when he had no immediate job to do. "Oddly enough, Doc," he had replied, "the last time I was up I was worried sick as to how I should have the squadron poodle cropped—we have a wonderful poodle, you know, pitch-black, called Puff, and the fellows had left it up to me."

I went back to my flat to have the last session with Messalina. It was half-past two, and I was a little tired. I walked slowly round the propped-up photographs, still bothered by unconscious murmurings. Finally I took the pair showing the severed Messalina head and sat down to examine them. These two pictures were perhaps the nearest of all to being duplicates; each showed a life-sized head from directly in front, held aloft by the headsman's hand grasping the hair. In both, the eyes were partly closed. But the Leder painting showed a face with the full red lips drawn down in almost a snarl; whereas in the Redel face the lips were drawn down in pain and the general expression of the face followed what I thought of as the familiar "martyrdom" lines. There was a difference in the grasping hand too; the Redel hand was a lighter, less hairy extremity. As I continued to examine this pair of pictures I was growingly aware of unanswered promptings on some deeper level of my mind. But I could do nothing more; I was too tired. So I gathered together the photographs, locked them up, and went to bed. I picked up my Thomas Browne to read a passage or two, but fell asleep with it still unopened in my hand.

13

It was a day of clear sky and blazing sun, and I turned in from the crowded Whitehall pavements with a considerable sense of inflated ego. I found myself hoping quite childishly that Cayley would be pleased with the stage I had reached with Messalina. "That," I said to myself sternly, "is quite enough for today's tribute to the father-figure; you are a big boy now."

I found only George Cayley in his office as I was shown in, and I was glad the meeting was to be between ourselves. He greeted me with the kind of expression that seemed to say he was expecting good, or at least interesting, news.

"I think, George," I started, sinking into one of his deep green chairs, "that at last we are on the way to solving the mystery of Monkey."

"Excellent; let me have your basic conclusions first, so that we have the business clear from the start." He sat back and closed his eyes.

"What I think can be taken as certainties are as follows," I said. "First, there is, or was, a Leder-Monkey artist we all know about. Second, there is a Redel artist quite distinct from him and yet closely related, both as to his reversed name and the similarity of the pictures. The similarity is so striking, yet so unmistakably different, that we must assume a close personal relationship existed, or possibly exists now, between the two—a relationship as between teacher and pupil, for example. Third—and I should not perhaps put this in as final, but I feel certain it is so—the Redel described by Joubert as the author of the pictures, and photographed by our man in Paris, is not the artist but probably a dope peddler. If I am right about that, he must be both agent and cover, in view of the signature. Agreed?"

Cayley nodded without opening his eyes.

"The reason I say this is because there seem to have been export stamps erased from the stretchers of the pictures, and because I am almost certain the artist works in Venice."

At this he opened his eyes. "That is an extraordinary discovery, Paul. How did you arrive at it?" And I told him of the night's work, and of the various conclusions I had come to.

"Of course," he replied, "this opens up all sorts of avenues, and it explains, I think, our friend Joubert's peculiar safe that Montgomery reported. He would seem to be in on a good thing—two good things, to be exact. He makes a profit on the pictures and a profit on drugs."

He went on. "What is particularly satisfactory is that I can now officially contact the French and Italian police on the drug aspect and so get a great deal of help without showing our real hand. I will do that immediately and tell them that both you and Montgomery are officially interested, so that you can receive all the help you want. We can also get confirmation of the Venetian source of the pictures now, because it will need only a simple check-up at the frontier to see if consignments of paintings have been coming through from Venice to Redel. There may, of course, be another middleman in Paris, but I doubt it."

142

"Yes, I doubt that too. What do you really think has happened to Monkey?" I asked. He leaned forward and drew triangles on his blotting paper for a minute or two. It occurred to me that it would be interesting to put Cayley through a Rorschach ink-blot test; it also crossed my mind that he had probably been through one anyway for the experience.*

"I should assume, I think," he said slowly, "that Monkey is dead; that is to say, if you are correct—and I feel sure you are—in saying definitely that there are two artists involved. And if that is so, if Monkey is indeed dead, the implications are not pleasant. The new artist, it would seem, must inevitably have been with him in Germany, was probably his pupil, and is now living and working in Venice. There are, of course, all kinds of unpleasant characters at large in Italy at the moment, and unless they are outstanding war criminals there is not enough time and manpower to track them down, or deal with them if they were traced. Next, it would appear that whoever continued Monkey's work must have been involved in his death. The Abwehr probably had their suspicions aroused by something or other and planted a competent art student on Monkey to keep watch. We know he took a number of pupils, so it would not have been difficult. Whoever it was must have taken over Messalina as model, but not, perhaps, as mistress. That might well account for what you call the changed attitude of the painter—the 'martyr approach,' I think you called it."

"But," I put in, "that brings us slap up against what is perhaps the chief mystery of all. Who is Messalina? Is she Helga Bamberg? Until now I think we have assumed too easily that they are one and the same person. At least I know

* I later found he had—"just to see what it was all about."

143

I have. We only know for a fact that there was a Helga Bamberg who assisted in torturing Caroline. Caroline's identification of her with the pictures does, I admit, seem excellent corroboration; but one cannot really be certain until Caroline gets a good view of her in person. I shall naturally try her with the photographs of the pictures, to get added confirmation."

"What about the times Caroline has seen her, or says she has seen her, in reality?"

"Good heavens above!" I said, interrupting him. "You remember I told you Caroline said she had seen Messalina in Chioggia? On the present evidence, the bloody woman may actually have been in Chioggia and have been seen by Caroline."

He nodded. "Yes, that might, in fact, be the first time she had really seen her after the war."

"Do you think perhaps it would now be worth while letting loose some of our people in Venice? They could be supplied with a set of Messalina portraits, and we could but hope she occasionally goes about the city. I can see no reason why she shouldn't; she has nothing to fear. All this is, of course, dependent on my Venice evidence being sound. What do you think? If we can pick her up, we can try and get proof of her identity and perhaps get a lead to her artist-protector at the same time."

"Yes. I think we will risk it. I will get the machinery moving. This whole case may be much more important than we yet know." He was obviously thinking far ahead of me, with his own special knowledge in mind.

"Without giving you the details," he went on, "I can say that for a long time we have known that there is quite a bunch of ex-German agents—as well as bigger cogs—in Venice. Money, I should imagine, is very short; and what could be better than drugs and pictures to supply their needs for the present? They will all, of course, find their way back to the Fatherland when it settles down, as every country can use good operatives."

"George, would you not think, from their point of view, that it was a bit risky doing those paintings in so similar a manner to Leder's? Wouldn't he be sure to attract our people's attention ultimately?"

"Oh, no; that was safe enough, really. If they had not been so foolish as to mix drugs with their painting—still assuming that lucky discovery of yours is correctly interpreted—they could go on indefinitely, even if we suspected that Monkey's death was connected with them. They would know they were not big enough fry to make it essential for us to track them down and deal with them in peacetime. And there is another point too. It would be purest chance if the pictures were ever to be seen by any of our people, as they go quickly from producer to consumer, or should do so. I imagine Joubert must be clear of the espionage racket, otherwise he would not show the Redel pictures in his shop, even for the short time he does. That practice of his is probably to keep his special clients perpetually uneasy as to their claims on the pictures, and also keep the prices up."

A telephone rang on George Cayley's desk. He picked up the red receiver, answered, listened, and suddenly looked troubled. With his hand over the mouthpiece, he turned to me. "Paul, it is Anne. Caroline is much worse. Will you talk to her—Anne, I mean?"

I took the phone from him.

145

"Paul," came Anne's distant voice from Garda, "Caroline has had a sort of relapse. She is very much like our first sight of her. It is, of course, that woman. No, she hasn't seen her again. It is the Chioggia incident. After leaving her alone for a bit, it has returned, and Caroline is more convinced than ever that it was Messalina she saw. I am certain she feels in real danger."

"Anne, I want you to do something very special. I want you to get down on paper the exact circumstances of the meeting, or the supposed meeting, in Chioggia. Take Caroline over and over the incident; make her try and remember every detail of clothing and so on. Also question her about the apparently slight effect it seemed to have on her at the actual time she saw Messalina. Then add what you remember yourself. I shall come out to Garda tomorrow—I'll fly to Milan, if you can get me picked up there with the car."

Anne then asked about suicide, and I told her not to worry too much about that, as it was not at all likely in Caroline's case. I told her how far she could go with the drugs I had left with her, saying that it would be best to keep Caroline exceedingly dopey until I arrived.

"George," I said after Anne had rung off, "I'm afraid we have a pretty sick girl on our hands again. Of course she might now, with this new bout, cooperate and give me a chance to do something for her. The more I think of it, the more I feel that she did see Messalina. If so, Messalina would definitely seem to be Helga. I do pray that Caroline will help me, and not hinder her treatment. I have often thought of sending her to another psychiatrist, but probably neither you nor she would agree—you for Service reasons, and she because she is convinced that all psychiatrists are sex-mad materialists. My God, she can make me furious with her at times. If only she would unbend!"

"Poor Paul," said Cayley. "It is ironical that the very qualities which make her so valuable to us are now making it so hard for her to be cured. But I am sure you will succeed."

He paused, and when I looked at him I was almost alarmed. His usually round and placid face was drawn into the nearest approach to hate that I had ever seen in it. He spoke very quietly, even for him. "Paul, I remember your saying that if you could give Caroline actual proof of Helga's death it might cure her."

I was suddenly bristling with apprehension. Could he have guessed what I intended?

"Yes, I did say that," I answered. "But the proof would have to be conveyed emotionally as well as logically; although I believe she has some power, very poorly developed in most people, to carry a logical fact over into the emotional field and make it work there."

"What I was wondering, Paul, was, if we catch up with Helga-Messalina, would it be possible to fake some photograph that might persuade Caroline that she was dead? The chances of the two ever meeting would be almost infinitesimal."

I breathed more freely. Cayley had advanced a perfectly feasible theory of action, and one we might well consider. I told him it could be done, and said that we must prepare for such a chance. Privately I was determined that Helga should die in reality, if indeed she were alive. The chance, no matter how slight, that any temporary cure might be later undone, was too dangerous to play with.

"I'm glad you think so, Paul. I must work out the whole thing—as it touches personnel—while you are off to Garda. I will lay on the Venice observers immediately, and get in touch with the Italian customs people. Whoever I put in charge of that side will make contact with you later—if, that is to say, anything at all does happen. I think Montgomery might be the best man for the job, after he has finished with Redel in Paris. In case I have to put a temporary man in Venice, you had better give me a contact quotation from your favourite doctor for identification."

So I gave him this sentence from Sir Thomas Browne: "The created world is but a small parenthesis in Eternity."

"He will introduce himself," said Cayley, "with that quotation and with the code-word for the day. Meanwhile both you and I will want a lot of photo-printing done. If you will get your Messalina negatives and take them to the Yard, I will get the fellows there to do an all-night job on them. Say what you want for showing to Caroline, and select half a dozen or so portraits of Messalina which could be isolated and enlarged as identification aids to our observers—and, Paul, let me have a full report on Caroline as soon as you can."

When I walked down the Home Office steps and out into the sunshine I felt oddly disjointed in mind. The Caroline case would have been of nightmare quality to many people, and would have disgusted or otherwise upset them. Since disgust is seldom experienced by a psychiatrist, except perhaps when cracking a rotten egg, it was not so much distaste that beset me as a feeling of unease and unreality. Were it

148

not for the very real Caroline, were it not for her being in danger from the fantasy world, I would have gladly consigned the whole business, including the solution of Leder's fate, to perdition, and asked George Cayley to take me off the case. But Caroline's life now literally seemed to depend on me, and I realized—to make it worse—if that life was to be saved it would depend more upon my luck than upon my skill.

It was through no conceit of my powers that I was determined to carry on. I was quite simply convinced in my own mind, no matter how irrationally, that we should stumble upon the solution, and that such a solution to Caroline's trouble was necessary on quite a low level of mentality.

If I could be the means of releasing her from the bogey of Helga-Messalina, it was not my business what she did with her life afterwards. For there is, or should be, a clear realization in the mind of every psychiatrist where his prerogative ends. It ends with freeing his patients from bondage, and does not continue into the sphere of telling them what to do and where to go afterwards. If we are then asked to take a further part in our patients' lives, it should be only to help them reach a place of their own choosing, and not to choose the place for them. The latter is a responsibility commonly usurped by their friends and relations and those demented dogmatists who are so uncertain of their own destinations that they feel they must coerce everybody else.

As I floated off to sleep that night I was far ahead of events. Caroline had been cured in my imagination, and I was waiting, fascinated, to see what she would choose to do with herself. I vaguely remember associating this thought with the memory of a dear but distracting friend of mine who was once choosing a hat in Bond Street. I had stood by, not saying a word, but praying she would decide on the one I wanted her to have. Finally, of course, she chose something quite different.

14

It was a bumpy flight until we were well over the Alps, and this seemed to presage the days ahead. I could only hope that the smoother passage over north Italy and the safe routine landing at Milan were as good an omen for the more distant future.

As the plane lurched to a stop on the concrete apron, I caught sight of a familiar figure leaning on the rail. It was Nellie, and I was delighted to see her.

"Nellie, my dear," I said when we were finally on our way out to the car, "you are an angel to come yourself. Now I can really lie back and be uninhibited all the way to Garda —unless you've brought anyone else?" I added hastily.

"No, Harvey, I wanted you to myself. I feel a little too rarefied at the moment."

"And you need, I hope, some good vulgar company," I added. She looked very charming in a kind of semi-dirndl turn-out, and as we set off from the airport in the blazing sun I felt happy and relaxed for the first time in weeks. I resolved that we would not talk about Caroline, and for the whole of that drive we just batted around any and every topic that drifted by. Pictures, travel, drink, philosophy, fiction, sex, and the kinds of Italian petrol available—all of them came our conversational way and were dealt with lazily and pleasantly. The great joy of talking to Nellie was that

151

one need never be on guard against saying the wrong thing, the inappropriate thing, or the embarrassing thing. She took life as it came and was far too mature to wrestle with the inevitable or get anxious about the trivial. I think those few hours did more to refresh me than a whole holiday would normally achieve.

Only as we came in sight of her beloved Villa Campagnola amid its protective cypress trees did I mention Caroline.

"You will find her in a poor way, Harvey. I think you will have to do something drastic."

"Is she being a great burden to you and George?" I asked.

"Burden? No, not at all. It is only that she now emanates such a strong current of fear and unease. But luckily George doesn't notice it, and we can cope. Anne, of course, is splendid. I wish to goodness that young woman would up and marry some good, straight, normal man. She deserves—how do you half-Americans say, Harvey?—a break."

"She probably will marry some day; but her private life is a closed book to George Cayley and me. That is to say, if she has any. We give her absolute hell at times, and never by so much as a murmur does she reveal annoyance or exasperation."

"She's terribly fond of you, Harvey. You should hear the nice quiet things she says about you sometimes; and she says them, I'm glad to say, in front of Caroline too."

"Yes, bless her; but I hope she says them in front of Caroline to offset that strange woman's suspicion of me. But seriously, I know Anne is fond of me, and loyal; but I suspect, mercifully for us all, that her equal affection for Cayley keeps her from overmuch concentration on either of us. I think it's mostly rather filial, and she probably has a stack of boy friends at her beck and call."

As I said this we turned into the villa drive and saw Anne herself coming towards us. But it was a more worried-looking Anne than I had ever seen before.

"Oh, Paul, I am glad to see you. I've been so worried I don't know what to do. It's not that I'm afraid Caroline will harm herself or anything, but to see her back where we found her—and after all the hopes we had!"

Anne and I walked slowly between the olive trees while Nellie garaged the car.

"Have some tea first, Paul, and then come and see her. I'll go up and tell her you will be with her in a few minutes."

I had a quick tea with Nellie and George and then went up the shallow marble stairs. I felt heavy and defeated, and even the long drive with Nellie seemed far away as I knocked on the door. Anne opened it and took me across the bedroom and out onto the balcony—a balcony I had so often sat on and from which I had gazed across at the blue water and the blue mountains beyond.

Caroline lay in a steamer chair, her head back and her whole body in an uncomfortable posture of exhaustion. She turned her head and smiled as I came out through the glass door. I was again struck, as I always was, with the beauty and depth of character in her face. But now it seemed almost submerged beneath a filmy surface of pain and terror.

I stood by her and picked up her hand, a gesture of mixed feelings on my part—of affection for her, of sorrow, and perhaps of determined hope. I held her hand and looked at her. She had laid her head back on the cushion and sighed, but I had the distinct idea that, no matter how much she had resisted me in the past, she was still in need of me and was glad to have me back. It might be she was so miserable that she clutched at any straw, even me.

I sat down and then lay back on a chair beside her, and for some minutes neither of us said a word. I was gazing over at the mountains above Limone, and my mind was a blank. I had no plans for Caroline, no strategy; I was waiting as much for a prompting from deep within myself as I was for her to start speaking.

Finally I turned my head and found her looking at me with her strained, troubled eyes. "Dr. Harvard," she said, "do you mind if I call you Paul, as Anne does?"

"Of course, Caroline. I should be delighted. After all, I have called you Caroline all this time."

From an irresolute dreamer I had suddenly become my professional self again. My job was to get this woman better. If I was to do any good I needed evidence and cooperation. Why, then, did she ask that question now? From the various motives that might have prompted it I was inclined to choose fear. She was bereft of her protective covering and she wanted support. To move from "Dr. Harvard" to "Paul" was to come symbolically nearer to a possible source of security—her antagonism to me was at present swamped by fear.

"Caroline, before we talk about Helga Bamberg, tell me something about your attitude to me, or rather to psychiatrists. When did you set yourself against us? As a profession, I mean. Or is it me as a human being that you are opposed to?"

"I am deeply sorry, Paul, for some of the things I have said to you," she answered. "I have thought a lot about my attitude to you, and I believe, if I am honest with myself, it was what Dennis told me about his experiences with psychiatrists that must have influenced me."

"What did he tell you, and when?"

"He had come to dine with my parents and me, and something to do with psychology cropped up in our conversation. This started Dennis off on a long attack based on what he had seen of psychiatrists in the war. His two main points seemed to be that they were materialistic to a degree, and often worse; and that they defended the cowards. I knew nothing about the subject, and I suppose that my respect for his opinions put me against the whole thing. And then, so soon afterwards, I became ill, and Sir George put me in your charge. It seemed like some terrible judgment on me; I had, so to speak, got what I deserved."

"Caroline, what happened was, amongst other things, that you came naturally to associate me with both materialism and cowardice. In other words, the man who was supposed to cure you was automatically an enemy of your religion. And to make it worse, since you linked psychiatrists with the defence of cowards, you were by implication one of the cowards. So you had to resist me in both my roles, because if you did not resist, you would feel guilty all round; and you were determined at all costs not to fall into my power." I paused, but she said nothing. So I went on.

"Do you see a little more clearly now, Caroline, that it was me as a symbol and not as a person that you were against? Do you think you feel more able to cooperate now? You know, I am sure, that between us we could get you out of all this and make you free to do whatever you wish?"

"Yes, Paul, I think I am getting more sensible. What you

155

said just now about my reaction to you was rather a shock; but I feel deep down that you are right."

Then I asked her to describe in detail her recent meeting with Messalina at Chioggia. It appeared that Caroline, Anne, and the Langleys were strolling along by the little harbour, admiring the orange-brown sails of the fishing boats, and George was just telling them the origins of the great eyes which were painted on the bows of every ship. They came to a standstill at that point, and Caroline looked up and across one of the boats to the other side of the narrow seaway. She found herself staring at a big woman who was dressed in rather an "arty" way, as she described it. The woman was in profile and was talking to a man. Caroline immediately felt the familiar and chilling fear she had experienced before, but not nearly as strongly. She remembered saying to herself that it was only a resemblance, and was probably some quite different woman anyway. After all, there was quite a distance between them. As she was reasoning with herself like this, a group of tourists came between them, and at the same time the woman began to walk slowly away. She was lost to view behind sails and rigging. Caroline had been so actively trying to argue herself out of her fears, and indeed was so successful, that she had noticed very little in the way of detail, except that Messalina had on a réd frock with some sort of pattern on it; that was all.

So efficiently had she coped with the situation at the time that she neither showed any outward sign, nor mentioned the incident to Anne until they were back at the villa. Then she did feel rather depressed and told Anne of the incident. Apparently the telling helped to back up her brave reasoning. It was not until some time afterwards that the delayed-action anxiety had started to plague her in earnest, and finally I had been sent for.

At this point I fetched some photographs of the Messalina pictures and showed them to her. All of them, she said, were of Helga. She was quite certain.

We talked all round the subject of Messalina, and Caroline seemed to gain a little liveliness. Among the points I asked her to consider was the question of what she, Caroline, actually saw as happening to her if Messalina was really on her track. And Caroline ultimately said in rather a surprised voice, "Well, I suppose the worst that could happen to me would be that she would kill me—and I don't suppose that would matter. You know, Paul, I never thought of that before; it is rather a comforting idea and almost takes the horror out of my fear of her."

"Caroline," I asked casually, "what sort of evidence do you think would eliminate your fears of Helga? I mean, in your imagination. If, for example, you saw a report of her death, with a photograph of her after she had been knocked down by a car, or whatever caused her end—would that, do you think, weigh with you?" I hoped no faltering of eye or voice betrayed how much her answer would mean.

She looked up at the sky and said slowly and thoughtfully, as if she were acting out the imagined situation to see how it felt, "Oh yes, I think that would be a very powerful blow to the fears, provided, of course, I recognized her without doubt in the photograph." She paused. "It would be like a less intense version of actually seeing her dead, which I suppose is what my mind and imagination crave for." Then another and longer pause. She turned her head towards me. "Paul," she said at last, "it just came to me that I want desperately to kill that woman myself—I don't think I've ever really realized that before, far less been able to say it."

"I'm glad you have," I answered. "It may mean that some of your fears of Helga were that she would retaliate against you for your unconscious but very understandable desire to kill her. The more you realize and bring into the open how much you want to kill her, the better. As your moral character would stop your doing it, even if you had the chance, it would be almost—if not quite—as good if someone else did the job, provided you had the proof, wouldn't it?"

She nodded. "Yes, that is exactly what I feel."

I did not mention one of my basic fears—that Helga Bamberg was already dead, and that we might never be able to demonstrate the certainty of her death. But the probability of her continued existence, I was thankful to realize, had risen steadily with our accumulating evidence.

Over the next few days I had several long sessions with Caroline, and I was delighted to see that she was visibly improving. The others noticed it too, and I felt that we were turning another corner.

We were idling down at the villa's bathing place when Bianca brought me a registered letter. I thanked her and put it down beside me on the hot paving stones. I was at the moment reluctant to break the spell of contentment that rested on me. I lay with my head in the shadow of a small clump of cypresses, and as I looked over the shimmering water towards Riva, two heads, and then bodies, rose up to block my view. Anne and Caroline were climbing out of our enclosed pool, dripping with water.

The wet, and very thin, swim suits clung tightly to their bodies, and I realized it was the first time I had ever seen

158

Caroline undressed, as it were. The sight of her made me catch my breath. She had a very seductive figure, a figure which I somehow felt was out of place in company with what I knew of her mind. When I analysed the feeling a little more honestly I realized I was almost angry at the thought that that body was not being shared as it should be for love and procreation.

Even more penetrating analysis on my part revealed that this physical—this sexual—impact on me had shaken the self-complacency with which I had regarded my relationship with Caroline. I was so sharply attracted physically that I saw myself in peril of fusing the appeal of spirit, mind, and body, and falling helplessly in love with her. It was a new and unwelcome complication in my life, and I was clearly conscious of fighting the attraction I found before me.

I picked up the letter and ripped it open. It was from George Cayley and carried curious news. First of all, I was right about Venice. The customs people there had confirmed my supposition, but the address they had recorded for the sender of the paintings proved a blind. The address was real enough, but no one there knew anything about any pictures. So Redel had been wisely taking precautions, presumably because of the drugs. Cayley said the Venice police were now very interested and were making inquiries. But there was no news of Messalina in Venice. This did not mean very much as yet, because the watchers had been on the job for only a short while, and Messalina might simply have missed passing near any of them or been indoors for a time. She might also have been away from the city. It had occurred to Cayley that she might even live in Chioggia, or somewhere on the Venetian mainland, so a check was being made in the most likely places. All this would take time, but there was no especial hurry.

I looked around me, relieved at not having to leave the villa yet. The two girls were now stretched out in the unshaded sunlight. George was asleep in a deck chair with a white hat pulled down over his face. Nellie lay on her orange bathing towel, talking across to the girls. When she heard me put down my letter she looked round, rolled over onto her stomach, and propped her head in her hands.

"Bad or good news, Harvey?" she asked.

"Neither, my dear; just a report. Thank heavens it is not a summons to leave your oasis. But I shall probably have to go to Paris or London soon for a few days. You will then have some peace."

It was just a week later, and we were in very much the same positions by the bathing pool, when Bianca came again with an envelope for me. But this time it was a telegram. It read:

CAN YOU GO PARIS TOMORROW STOP JAMES WANTS YOU URGENTLY STOP BAUDELAIRE.

"Baudelaire" was the day's code-word. I wondered what could possibly be urgent now where James Montgomery was concerned, for it was from Venice that we expected news.

15

One of my favourite travel habits is to sit lazily pecking at a light meal in the dining car of any train running amidst mountains. I suppose it is the combination of lulling movement, food, and the wonderful sensation of looking up at the great massive shapes or down at the steep valleys that gives me such acute pleasure. Then the railway itself is so satisfying, with its curiously predestined movement, running surely and safely through the precipitous landscape.

I had chanced to mention this to Caroline some days before I left Garda; and before I climbed into the car beside George Langley to start for Verona, she drew me aside and we walked a few steps up the drive.

"Paul," she said a little shyly, and ducked her head, "you remember what you said about loving to sit in the dining car looking at your favourite Swiss mountains?" I nodded.

"Well, would you promise me to keep this letter unopened until you are in the dining car in Switzerland?" She handed me a letter as she spoke.

"I'll do the next best thing, Caroline. The Simplon-Orient Express goes through at night, so I will read it at Domodossola when we stop before going through the tunnel. It must be a very sweet letter if you want it associated with that journey."

I waited until the train stopped that night at the frontier.

There was a full moon and a clear sky, and the great dark mountains made a mighty background to the scene. I stood on the deserted platform amidst the grandeur and the sharp silence of the Alps, and read Caroline's letter by the light of my pocket torch. It was one of the most charming letters I have ever received. I am not going to reproduce it here, except for a line or two.

"The last of my gratitudes," she wrote, "is that you have made me exchange a preoccupation with resisting you for a determination to get better, no matter what it costs my pride."

For those words, apart from the natural satisfaction that sincere flattery provides, I was profoundly grateful as a doctor. In whatever lay ahead we should at least be able to count on a positive attitude on Caroline's part, and that is often halfway towards winning the battle.

James Montgomery met me at the Gare de Lyon, and we took a taxi into the surging cacophony of the Paris streets. I could not help wondering, as our charioteer urged us along, how many taxis at that moment were occupied by people bent on such seemingly improbable business as ours. The flat two-dimensional mood of unreality often descended on people in our profession, as many members of the Service had told me.

James's news bothered and puzzled me. "Doctor," he had said, "someone has tried to murder Redel and probably succeeded. He was found stabbed in the back and floating in the Seine. A police launch must have spotted him very soon after he was attacked. They hauled him out and took him to hospital. That's all we know at the moment."

"But how did you find this out?"

"Well, our men saw him go out two nights ago and followed him. But he gave them the slip, and they reported to me immediately. I told them to go back and watch the flat. He did not come back that night, and next morning I saw this in the paper." He handed me a cutting. It read:

Late last night the body of a young man named Jean Redel was found by the police, floating in the Seine. He had been stabbed in the back. The police took him to hospital, and he is not expected to recover. The authorities believe the crime to have been committed only a few minutes before the unfortunate man was found.

"There can only be one explanation of that," I said. "He must have been attacked by the real Redel, the Redel who actually painted the pictures."

"Why?"

"I imagine that the pseudo-Redel—our young man in the Seine—found out about our interest in him; and Joubert may, for example, have showed him some of our photographs. Whatever it was, our man probably felt that discretion was called for temporarily, and sent a routine message to Venice for his genuine namesake to stop shipments either of pictures altogether, or of drug-bearing ones. He might even have realized he was being watched, James. That is more than likely, especially if he deliberately threw off your people that night. I am sure it is the drug business that he felt was in danger."

"Then I suppose the real Venice Redel took it seriously enough to come to Paris to see what was happening."

"Yes," I said, "that is what I feel happened. When the two met, the Venetian probably thought our friend had outlived his usefulness and eliminated him. After all, it would be comparatively easy to get a new Paris agent and cover combined. Venice is clearly taking no chances."

"I wonder if by any chance the Paris police had had dealings with Redel before, recognized the photo you sent, and went round to make inquiries. That would have scared him even more than our men."

"That is certainly possible, and we shall soon find out. Did you talk to Sir George?"

"Yes. He said he would like to speak to you on the phone as soon as you arrived."

I had a full discussion with Cayley an hour later. He said he had already told the Paris authorities that James and I had an official police status, and they were waiting for us to contact them. He gave me full authority to do what I thought best at the moment. The first thing to be done was to ring Superintendent Claudel at the Quai des Orfèvres and make an appointment to see him. Within half an hour James and I were being shown into his austere office on the Ile de la Cité.

Claudel and I were old friends, and his tall lanky figure always struck me as oddly un-French. Perhaps we are too used to fictional French detectives, who are generally stout and perspiring. He shook hands, and we said how pleased we were to see each other. Then he introduced us to Inspector Blanchard, who was the head of their "dope squad," as the Americans say.

"Dr. Harvard"—he always pronounced it "Ah-varr"— "I had expected to see you before. One of our men mentioned you some short time ago in connection with examining a shop window in the dark." His eyes almost danced with enjoyment of his little joke, and I spoke very apologetically.

"It was very impolite of me not to have called on you then, Superintendent, but I was only fencing in the dark; and it is as a result of that—er—'escapade,' shall I call it, that my friend Montgomery and I are here now."

"Ah, but you must not take it seriously, what I say. But what is this interesting business you are on? Sir George tells me that you were working on a psychological investigation when you stumbled on a matter which now interests us here, and that we can deal with you instead of our other colleagues at Scotland Yard."

"Yes, but I am really only handing over to you. My professional interest is nearly satisfied," I said.

I then told him of my discovery of the powder behind the Redel picture, of our suspicion that Joubert might be involved—omitting any reference to the wall safe—and that we had seen that the police had dragged a certain Redel from the Seine with a knife in his back. Finally that we believed it was the same Redel we were concerned with.

"But I fear he is probably dead by now, from what the newspapers said," I added.

"Dead, eh? We will soon check up on that." He rang through to one of his assistants and told him to see what the news was on a man named Redel. "That man was the subject of a Scotland Yard inquiry recently, was he not?" he asked. I nodded. "I don't think we had anything against him, anyway," added Claudel.

We talked of various trivialities for the next few minutes, and then the conversation came back to drug-smuggling, and the method of putting the stuff behind pictures.

"Have you ever come across that method of smuggling before, Monsieur?" I asked Inspector Blanchard.

"No, Doctor, we haven't—and we are very interested. But we did once find a man who laid the powder on his canvas with a binding medium and then painted modernistic pictures on top of it; it was most ingenious, especially as paintings of that kind are often crude in handling and done with heavy impasto. But a false lining—that is another change rung on the theme."

Claudel's telephone rang. He lifted the receiver, listened, frowned, told the caller to wait by his instrument, and rang off.

"Dr. Harvard, there has been an odd development in the case of our man Redel. He has escaped!"

"Escaped?" I echoed in amazement. "But surely he was stabbed in the back?"

"Yes, he was. The story is odd. Our men took him to hospital, and it appeared he was not badly hurt at all—the knife did not go in very far, and not into a vital place at that. He felt very shaken up, or pretended to; but the hospital authorities said he would be able to leave in a day or two anyway. Meanwhile Redel—who said he was an artist—had given a statement to our men which had satisfied them. His story was common enough. He had picked up a girl, and they had gone down to that riverside pavement below the Quai de Béthune, which is on the Ile Saint-Louis. But she must have been in league with a crook, as a man followed them down and accosted him. As his back was turned to the girl he felt a sharp pain, and, realizing that he had fallen among thieves, dived into the river and was lucky enough to be picked up by our people. He said they must

166

have known he had a good deal of money on him—he had just been paid for a picture—and that was true. He had fifty thousand francs in his pocketbook. So our men were satisfied; they couldn't do anything about it anyway, and so left him alone at the hospital. Last night, after lights were out, he quietly got up and left the hospital without anyone being the wiser. You see, as he was brought in by the police he had been put in a separate room, so it was easier than ever after our men left."

"Well," I said, "that is a very curious development. Do you think it is worth searching his flat and Joubert's office? But that is your affair. He may, of course, be back at his flat." I was secretly cursing our lack of precautions in calling off our own watchers after hearing he had been stabbed; we should have to rely on the police to tell us if he had come back.

"Yes, we will do that and more. We cannot send out a general call for him and pull him in, as we have nothing against him except your finding of the powder—and that, of course, is not evidence to us. We have, however, grounds for suspicion. So we will search the flat, question him if he is there, and go after Joubert at an opportune moment." He turned to his colleague. "Will you see to that, Blanchard? Dr. Harvard can save you a little by giving you the address."

I told Blanchard the number in the rue de l'Estrapade, and, after saying a friendly adieu to James and myself, he left.

"Ah, Monsieur," I said, "I am glad he is gone, as I can now give you the background which I am sure you suspected." Claudel nodded and smiled.

"The reason my friend here and I were originally interested in Redel was because we thought he might be an agent our people once employed in Germany, who was an artist, and who had disappeared some time ago. We saw some of his pictures by accident, and they were oddly similar to those our man had done. I came in on the psychological side—or the artistico-psychological side, shall we say—and we were simply trying to contact the artist. This was not at all easy. All his work was sold through Joubert, and he would not put us on to him, ostensibly because he thought we would then try to deal direct, and he would lose his other clients and the sales commission. Then by a stroke of luck we got a line on Redel just as we thought we were in a blind alley. The next thing we know is the newspaper announcement."

"Very odd and very interesting," said Claudel. "I think in that case we had better make a wary but thorough search for him if he is not at his flat."

This put us in a dilemma. I hoped to goodness that the search would not get under way too soon, because I had wanted Redel to lead us to the real artist. When we thought he was dead it had seemed the end of our hopes, and naturally James and I would have concentrated on Messalina in Venice. Now it was still worth using our Paris Redel as a stalking horse, especially as I was so sure he would lead us to Venice—unless, of course, he was so badly scared that he wanted to disappear entirely.

In either case I wished Claudel would ease up on the chase. But I could say nothing. So we soon took our leave and walked out into the warm night air and into the historic surroundings of the Police Judiciaire. I was glad that James Montgomery was as romantic about scenery as I was. We walked the few steps along the island to look at Notre Dame, which was very cleverly floodlit. Hackneyed a sight as it may be, the cathedral is always just as glorious a Gothic sight to me as if no tourist had ever set eyes on it. As we stood gazing at its ghostly façade I seemed to drift back through time like the true sentimental American I am—or rather, half-American.

"Let's go over to the Left Bank, James, and look at those cunningly lit flying buttresses."

So we sauntered over the Pont Saint Michel and along the Quai Montebello to where the view was best. We leaned on the balustrade and admired the sight in silence.

"James," I asked, after a minute or two, "you got on to our people in Venice and warned them that our Paris Redel is another possible lead if he arrives?"

"Yes, Doctor; and I sent off three of the miniature photographs this morning. Of course he may already have got there. Or he may have gone underground here, or in Belgium, to let his attacker think he's dead. I was afraid for a moment that the story of his escape from the hospital might get into the papers. But I read them fairly carefully, and I've seen nothing. It would not be much to anyone's credit —or interest—to announce it anyway, so we can suppose the attacker thinks his victim dead."

We chatted on inconsequentially for some time and then fell silent, both of us lost in the scene before us. Then a party of young Englishwomen came by, accompanied by an elderly woman. They were talking excitedly and broke rudely into our contemplations. The spell broken, we idly turned our heads and watched them retreat along the pavement.

"How dreadfully the young women of today walk," I said. "They either swing along like soldiers, slouch like spivs, or sway like tarts."

"Good for you, Doctor—I must remember that. Did you make that up as you went along, or had you thought it all out beforehand? But you're quite right, all the same."

"As a matter of fact, it came out quite spontaneously. I was thinking how beautifully Caroline walked and moved."

"Caroline?" he asked. "Who's she?"

I had forgotten for the moment that he did not know about Caroline. "Oh," I said, "she is a patient of mine, a very lovely woman."

16

I was in a state of semi-suspended animation; I could not work, I could not play. And I think George Cayley was in nearly as bad a condition. A week had passed since James Montgomery and I had learned of the attack on Redel and his disappearance. I had left James in Paris and come back to London to await events. Then silence. No news came from Venice; nothing from Paris. After two days we sent James to take over in Venice so that he could be as near as possible to where we thought our quarry, or quarries, operated.

Regular reports from Anne showed, I was thankful to see, that Caroline was greatly improved and was back to what I thought of as her standard "subnormal" state. That is to say, she was depressed and anxious but not acutely and incapacitatingly so.

After five days we got an interesting report from Paris. The police had searched Redel's flat without result and had temporarily called off their search for him. But Joubert had been caught with a sizable hoard of heroin in his safe. For a moment I felt sorry for him, but anyone dealing in drugs is compounding the devil's felony and should be put out of business and out of circulation. It was significant that he did not implicate Redel, whose address and accounts in Joubert's books referred only to the profitable transactions in art.

At the end of the week I rang up George Cayley and asked him round for dinner. We talked trivialities during the meal, and it was not until Sarah brought our coffee that we became serious. I then suggested my going to Venice. There at least I should be nearer the centre of things and could find enough to take my mind off the case until something happened—if anything ever did.

"You know," said Cayley, "I seldom remember any case in which I have felt more frustrated. We don't really know what we're investigating, or whom, and we only know that we want certain information about two people, both of whom may well be dead. And yet I am sure that we are right to pursue it to the end, although I admit that it may not have an end. I would not mind even that, were it not that Caroline's health, and with it the work we want her for, depends on the outcome. We are, of course, also interested in what happened to Leder. As to your going to Venice, I think it would be a good thing; it would be good for you in your present state, and good for the work to have you on the spot with young Montgomery."

"I think I shall be off as soon as I can," I answered. "Probably tomorrow, if I can get an air booking. Incidentally, it will be an advantage being only a few hours' car journey from Caroline. I think she is definitely better, but one simply cannot tell with her at present. By the way, have you seen her parents recently?"

"Yes, I have been down there twice during the past few weeks, and they are puzzled but resigned about the whole business. Caroline writes to them every so often and tells them she is having a restful time, and that seems to satisfy them after a fashion."

"And about me?" I asked. "I hope I don't figure as too much of an ogre in the family?"

"Young Newcomen helped there. At first, when he traced you in Wimpole Street, he made them suspicious and unhappy with his news. But of course he was very upset himself. Then he apparently blew your trumpet very flatteringly after your meeting, and I tried to complete the good work by saying you were safe and solid, and that I had known you for years."

"Do you know if Newcomen gets letters from her, George?"

"No, I don't know. I met him at the Nortons' the last time I was there, and I have the impression that he accepts the situation, whatever it is, so far as he and Caroline are concerned. So I should rather imagine she does write occasionally, but keeps him at the usual friendly arm's length. I like him."

The airlines were booked up, so I thumbed a lift in an R.A.F. Dakota as far as Milan. It was an uneventful journey, and I was feeling fresh and rested when I climbed aboard a local train there for the short journey to Venice.

As we ran through the hot flat landscape towards Verona I sent as many silent greetings to Lake Garda as my limited psychic equipment would allow. When the train finally drew into the terminus at Venice, the afternoon light was failing, and the charm of the place was upon me. I do not care a fig for the disillusionists—I know all about the smells and the peeling pink plaster and the wretched motorboats that are spoiling the canals. But the charm holds for me, chiefly, I must admit, for romantic reasons.

I waited while the crush of passengers slowly dissolved

from the station and then took a gondola. The journey down the Grand Canal is for me an ever-fresh experience, with its colourful traffic rocking by, the crowded *vaporetti*, and the architectural variegation of the buildings as they sit serenely behind their painted mooring-poles. Tonight the weather promised to be glorious, and I decided not to contact James Montgomery yet; this evening I would have to myself.

After cleaning up at the Danieli I had dinner and set off for a round of the things everyone does—or should do—during a Venetian evening. I first wandered about the crowded Piazza and had a drink at Florian's. Then, as night came across the lagoons and gently covered the canals and campanili, I hired a gondola and told its pilot to take me out to the concert party, which held court in a barge on the lagoon near San Giorgio. They played all the old hackneyed tunes, including, of course, "Ciribiribin"; and I just lay there on the cushions and indulged unashamedly in nostalgia. Twenty years ago a very aloof, very beautiful girl had sat there in a gondola with her chaperon, listening to the same music, and I had been on tenterhooks in another gondola, gazing at her. I had been introduced to her only the day before.

By nine o'clock next morning James, who had walked over from his hotel, had told me over breakfast how our watchers were organized and how they reported. There were not many of them, but they constantly threaded the city and its waterways, and Venice is not a very large place. There were also telephone points in certain private apartments. But, so far, nobody resembling the Paris Redel or Messalina had been seen.

"You know, James, I have a feeling Redel is not here yet, but that he will come. I may be quite wrong, but let's risk it."

174

'All right, Doctor, I will get a man full-time on the station, with reliefs, and on the landing at the Riva degli Schiavoni, where the Fusina boats come in. As I am sure his attacker thinks him dead, and Redel must obviously assume so too, I don't think he will go to the trouble of a very furtive entry. If he does, there are, of course, a hundred ways in. By the way, we ought to make ourselves known to the police straight away; they will know about us already."

For three days we roamed Venice either together or singly. For my part, I wanted to re-acquaint myself with the city. I not only refreshed my memory but learned the map of Venice off by heart, even to quite minor canals and *calli*. They were three uneventful days, but very profitably spent.

James decided to join me at the Danieli, as his own hotel was not very comfortable. So on the fourth day, after breakfasting together, we went out into the morning sun and walked towards the Piazzetta. The mood of my first night was still within reach, but the business we were about was effectively dispersing it.

"I shall be damned annoyed if this lovely place is going to be tainted for me with sordid associations. It looks as if it might," I added gloomily.

"Don't tell me you feel romantic about Venice too?" he said with genuine surprise.

"Romantic?" I answered. "My dear James, of course I do. I have just as many memories and illusions as the next man. Anyway, all Americans feel romantic about Venice."

We were off on foot to see the Church of S. Giovanni Crisostomo, near the Rialto Bridge, and we walked in a leisurely way, looking in shops and enjoying the noise and bustle. We left the church at about eleven and wandered along to the Rialto, intending to take a *vaporetto* back down the Grand Canal. The floating *vaporetto* station is just to the south of the bridge, and as we approached it we saw that one of those dirty little monsters was already alongside. We were in no hurry and decided to take the next one and to browse in the shops on the bridge meanwhile.

Just as we were turning away we heard a rising chatter of voices and some loud exclamations—no uncommon sounds in Venice. But I casually looked over my shoulder, and as if by some automatic mechanism my hand shot out and I gripped James's arm hard enough to make him wince.

It was easy to see the cause of the noise. The unwilling conductor of the *vaporetto* had lifted the gate and pulled a woman on board just as the boat began to move. The woman was Messalina.

"There she is!" I muttered. "Look, quick! On the *vaporetto*—the large woman who's just got on."

All we could do was look helplessly and desperately for a taxi motorboat. But there was not a vacant one to be seen.

"Oh, hell and damnation," said James. "Just our bloody luck—and we cannot get our people in time either."

"But wait a moment. That boat has got to get right round the big U-bend of the canal, with eight stops to make between here and San Marco. We can cut across easily in time to meet her. The only thing is that we could not get to any of those in-between stops in time, except perhaps Santa Maria del Giglio. But it's worth doing in case she stays on board. Let's go."

So we set off through the narrow passages and across the network of canals, making for the Giglio stop.

176

"Are you sure it was her, Doctor?"

"Absolutely. I don't think anyone could miss that face and figure. Those features we now know so well—the proud head, held high and haughtily, the near-sneer, the carriage of the body. It couldn't have been anyone else."

"To think that we so nearly had her," muttered James angrily. "It seems outrageously impossible that there—at this very minute—she is aboard that snuffling, filthy little boat and we can't get at her."

Three minutes later we came out onto the landing stage. James tapped my arm. "Here it comes now." It was madly tantalizing for us as we stood out on the landing stage, because the *vaporetto* had appeared round the bend and was pulling in to the Accademia stop on the other side of the canal. We could not possibly see who got off there. Three minutes later it moved off and headed towards us.

As it scraped alongside and the passengers disembarked, we examined everyone. Messalina was not among them. So James and I went aboard, and while the fussy little craft swam off on its next two stretches we moved about the deck checking the passengers. But our quarry was not to be seen, so we went and stood by the rail, despondently watching the pink and white façade of the Ducal Palace slide by, and oblivious to the beauty of the scene.

"That means," I said unnecessarily, "that she got off at one of the in-between stops. And they are on both sides of the canal. We can do nothing about it, of course, except curse our luck. But at least we are sure of one thing. Messalina is very much alive."

It was only a step from the San Zaccaria landing stage to

177

the hotel, and we went in out of the blazing heat—made much more uncomfortable by the glare from so much marble—and flopped down in the lounge.

"Damn and blast!" said James Montgomery, as he mopped his face viciously with his handkerchief.

For the next week we had no news of any kind. I took James to all my favourite haunts in Venice, and in the evenings we sat out under the stars or took gondola rides up the echoing canals. It was during one of these gondola journeys that we discussed the most difficult problem of our joint mission—the dealing with Messalina, if and when we found her. Following the plan I had pretended to agree on with Cayley, I told James that it was necessary to photograph a fake scene of her death before we handed her over to the police. I said that I did not know why Cayley wanted such a photograph, and that I had not inquired. James was well enough trained not to pursue this matter further.

We agreed that the ideal situation would be to wait until we could come upon Messalina alone and indoors. Then the essential move was to make her unconscious either by knocking her out or by the injection of some drug. It was important to have her unconscious long enough to fake her death scene for James to photograph. As my determination to kill her—seemingly by accident if it were possible, but outright if not—was adamant, I had to pretend a genuine interest in the faking scheme and put forward some plausible way of making her look really dead to the camera's eye.

We came to the conclusion that the best way to go about it was to imitate a death by stabbing. We would sprawl our unconscious prisoner in some stark and likely pose, cut a

178

couple of holes in her dress, and then soak the surrounding material with some dark liquid to simulate blood. We would then fix a stage dagger—we would have to find a good one—into one of the holes so that it appeared to be sunk deep into her body. Three or four photographs of such a scene, from various angles, could certainly be made convincing enough.

It was curious to lie in the darkness on the cushions of a gondola, under a Venetian moon, and discuss in whispers this real capture and unreal murder. As we went over the business in all its aspects, I had difficulty keeping my mind on the conversation. Little did James know that if we did get as far as cornering Messalina it would be a real corpse he would be called upon to photograph. I faced for the first time the implications of my determination to kill that woman. There had certainly been no melodrama in my mind when I decided to kill her, although I now realized I had always intended her death to look like an accident, or self-defence, if I could. About the ethics I had also decided. It was a ruthless criminal's life against Caroline's; that was justification enough for my action.

But now I was in the city in which the deed had to be done, and I had to think of hard facts. Just how did I intend to kill Messalina? But as I looked over towards the bustling life on the Riva, I again found it too theatrical a question to face now. "When I meet her I will do as the circumstances dictate," I said to myself. Then, almost as an afterthought, I decided to equip myself with a serviceable knife as well as the automatic I was carrying. That was as far as I would go this evening.

During the day we made a point of walking wherever we

could, so that our eyes were added to those of the watchers. And both day and night we left notice with our contact points of approximately where we were going, and at what times we would be at predetermined points. This was a laborious business, but we could take no risks.

On the seventh night James and I were being propelled along a labyrinth of silent canals by a herculean gondolier with very red lips and a very black moustache. The steel prow of our craft flashed in the gleam of passing lights, and the dilapidated but lovely palaces rose like a canyon on either side to show a highway of stars above us. Every few minutes we passed under a bridge and looked up into the faces of tourists leaning idly over the balustrades and gazing at us as we floated beneath them. For a moment their conversation would mingle with the rhythmical splashing of the single long oar; then silence again, except for the water noises, the oar splash and the gentle slip-slap of the little waves against the buildings as we passed their dark blank faces.

We had turned into the Rio di San Lorenzo, with the intention of emerging later on at the Schiavoni, and going thence to the concert party. We were gliding towards a bridge; James and I were silent, as we both liked this rather eerie form of night travel through the city.

We were just moving under the arch when a voice above us called out, "James!"

At once James turned to the gondolier and told him to pull in to the steps on the other side of the bridge. Then he called out, "Okay, Edward." We slid to a standstill by the wet marble, and a figure came down towards us. James got up from his seat, stood for a moment to gain his balance, and stepped onto the stairway. The two men spoke together, and James turned towards me.

"Doctor," he said, "our friend from Paris has arrived. One of our people has followed him to a hotel and has phoned us."

17

I climbed out of the gondola, and the three of us stood in the dark shadow of the bridge. Edward gave us the name of the hotel and where it lay. He said it was a rather sad little place near the Apostoli Church.

"Have you sent anyone there?" I asked.

"Yes, sir. There happened to be three of us at the telephone point—it's my flat, by the way—and I sent one of them straight there."

"Good. Now, James, everybody available can at last be deployed to cover our friend's movements. It might be as well if you got one of our people to move into the hotel if they have room—whoever is most suited by appearance and language to fit in there. I think it's worth the trouble, don't you?"

"Yes, Doctor, I think it is. It makes surveillance much easier for certain times of the day. Shall I organize a full series of reliefs and meet you, say, outside the Apostoli in half an hour? The hotel is only a few steps away."

"Yes. It is quite possible—even likely—that he will go after his quarry straight away, tonight. He probably won't risk being seen in daylight tomorrow before he can act. I imagine we can be sure that his visit to Venice is for unfriendly purposes. So let's get going. Edward, you had better come with me."

James paid off the gondolier, and we set out on foot.

Suddenly Venice had become a city of menace and foreboding. All its soft evening beauty was now lost on me. As we walked quickly along the narrow passages, across the bridges and echoing courtyards, the most curious memories and fantasies followed one another through my mind. I could remember, for example, a film I had seen years ago, a thriller, in which one was shown an aerial view of a city. The camera had then descended on the place as if the audience were in a diving aircraft speeding towards the buildings. Then the pace slackened; one approached a single building, then a window; and next one was through the window and looking over the shoulder of a man writing under a shaded light.

Tonight, if fortune was kind, we should be pinpointing two human bodies—perhaps three: the Paris Redel, the "true Redel," and Messalina. We crossed a small courtyard, dimly lit by one lonely lamp, and were swallowed up in the gloom of a passage.

After what seemed a tedious and lengthy walk we emerged into the piazza around San Canciano and crossed over the Apostoli canal. Five minutes later we were passing the side of the church, and I thought of the fine Tiepolo of Saint Lucy receiving the Sacrament, which was hanging so near us in the darkness of the Cornaro chapel.

We had waited in the shadows for about a quarter of an hour when James emerged from a passageway on the left and joined us.

"He is still safe in the hotel. I'll take you to a little café from which we can see our watcher. He will smooth down his hair if Redel comes out, and then we can follow." He

183

paused. "Doctor, I think only two of us—you and I—should follow our man, and we can call up reinforcements later if necessary. Do you agree?"

James had been thoroughly trained in all this practical part of our work, so I told him to take charge from now onwards. We sent Edward back to his flat to wait by the telephone for any emergency, and James and I sat down at one of the outside tables of a noisy little *trattoria*. We ordered some wine and settled down to wait. It was ten o'clock.

At midnight our fellow drinkers began to thin out, and when, at eleven minutes past the hour, James thought we had better move, I suddenly laid my hand on his knee. Our man had given the signal.

James leaned over to me and said quietly, "He is also making a sign that Redel is coming this way. So we'd better wait where we are."

A few minutes later a thin, dark man came towards us across the courtyard, making for a passageway which opened out of it to our right. He was easily recognizable as the Paris Redel from James's original photographs. He was walking slowly and deliberately. His face was a shadowy mask of determination and caution. We had arranged that James should actually shadow him, and I, who was not used to the technique, should keep James in view if I could. To make it easier to follow in the darkness of so many of the city's passageways, James was to drop silver-paper confetti, an idea we had tried out under various conditions during the past week.

James got up when Redel had passed, and sauntered away. Then I rose and followed.

In the state of mind I was in, it seemed to be an hour's

walk, but my watch showed it had been only twenty minutes as we passed the Church of San Rocco and made towards the Frari. We skirted that noble great building and almost at once were swallowed up by another of those deep canyon-like passages. We passed only a few hurrying figures at that time of the night, and I had the fleeting fantasy that each was on the way to commit a murder.

I could not hear James, nor could he hear me, as we both wore thick rubber soles, and in a particularly black cavern of a passageway I almost ran into him. He spoke in a whisper. "Doctor, he has gone into that courtyard ahead of us to the left—can you see it?"

I knew that James had very good night vision and that he had also been taking Vitamin A to improve it still further. But I could see only the slightest blur in the darkness ahead.

"Not clearly," I said, "but I think I can see a faint gap."

"I'm going in there. Give me a couple of minutes and follow, will you?"

The silence seemed to descend from the star-lit gap above and surround me like a wall of cellophane—I felt that what hemmed me in was invisible but impermeable.

I measured off the seconds and went forward. The court-yard seemed comparatively light when I reached the entrance, and I could see at once that there was an elaborate outside staircase like the one in the Palazzo Contarini. It would at least give us extra cover. I kept to the left-hand wall of the courtyard, and this time I saw James standing beneath the stairway.

"He has just gone up," he said. "I think two flights. Listen!"

There was a faint metallic sound above us, as if someone was gently trying a door handle. Then silence.

"These places," said James, "are probably large one-floor flats, with front doors on the landings, where once were open doorways. I'm going up to take my chance. I don't mind who finally get themselves killed, but first we want whoever is there for questioning. I will whistle softly when I'm up, if it is safe."

As James slid away and disappeared round the first pillar of the stairway, I could not help being troubled about the risk we were taking—the risk that the Paris Redel would kill the "real Redel" before we could stop him. If this happened, we should have to rely on the Paris Redel for locating Messalina, or else lie in wait for her here or elsewhere in Venice. Either way it seemed fairly sure that we should meet up with her in the end, but it might take a long time.

I could not hear a sound. I looked at the glowing dial of my watch and counted the minutes. Then a peculiar sound rustled down from above. I edged out from beneath the stairway and looked up. In the glimmer of the night sky I could see a figure climbing into a window on the second floor. It was the slight disturbance of the creeper that I had heard. I watched until the figure disappeared. Then there was a long silence. It was ten minutes before I heard a metallic sound. Then silence once more.

The courtyard lay around me like the bottom of a well, with the windows forming rectangles of deeper blackness in the surrounding gloom. The brilliant starlight above was the only comfort. I watched one particularly bright member of the heavens, and thought of its light coming to me over the æons.

186

Turning my head, I could see some of the stars reflected in a window above me. Reflecting windows formed a simple association in my mind with mirrors, and, quite suddenly, a vivid image leaped up from the unconscious and hung quivering in my mind's eyes. I could feel myself stiffening all over in a living rigor. For I now knew who the "real Redel" was; I knew who painted Joubert's pictures.

My first impulse was to run up the stairway and try to follow James into the building. But that impulse faded immediately, and I stood still. A faint whistle sounded from above. I moved out of my hiding place and went silently up the stairway until I caught sight of James standing in the far corner of a landing.

"Doctor, I am stumped for the moment. He had left this landing when I arrived, and I thought I heard him climbing upwards."

"I saw him get from the end of the balustrade into a window level with this landing," I whispered. I decided I would not at this moment tell James about my revelation.

"Ah," said James, "then that is all right. He was probably standing on the sill when I got here, and I'm damned glad I didn't show myself. Did he get right in?"

"Yes," I said.

"Okay, I shall go in now. It may be a bit difficult for you to follow, unless you are in good training, so it might be better for you to wait until I open the front door from inside."

He climbed onto the balustrade and moved slowly round the creeper-covered column and disappeared from my view. I could plainly hear the slight rustle of leaves in the stillness. Then silence again.

I leaned against the dark corner of the landing and tried to analyse my feelings. But the pressure of the moment kept all rational speculation away. All I could do was wait there in the darkness, wait for the large door to open and admit me to whatever was in store. I did not even guess what it might be.

I put my ear to the door and, hearing nothing, was just turning away my head when I thought I heard a weak cry coming from somewhere in the flat. I stood back in my corner and listened. Someone was unlatching the door from the inside, and he seemed in a hurry. I think I had automatically made up my mind that James would open the door quietly and surely, with no haste. But these sounds did not fit the pattern. So I flattened myself against the wall, turned my head towards the door, and transferred all my weight onto my toes.

The door opened, and a figure was outlined against the pale gloom of the marble landing. It was the Paris Redel.

I retained a few unpleasant parlour tricks from my Service training days; one of them was adequate for the present job. As Redel took his second step out onto the landing, I moved silently out of my corner and gave him a sudden push in the back, at the same time crooking my left leg round his. He stumbled, nearly recovered, and then pitched down the steps. As I ran down after him I pulled my long torch out of my pocket and, before he could recover, hit him hard over the head. I thought he had already hit his head on the steps, but I could take no chances.

My one idea was to get him back into the flat. So I grasped his legs, crouched, and with a heave pulled him over my

188

shoulders like a long sack. Then I staggered up the steps, across the landing, and into the hall.

I now felt sure he had attacked James and got the best of it; but Redel was my immediate concern. I locked the front door and used my torch to find the light switch, which I turned on. It must have taken a minute or two to find a mackintosh and strip off the belt, but Redel was still unconscious when I bent over him and tied his hands together. I was rather inexperienced in such matters, so, like a man who knows no knots, I was determined to intensify the tying up. I soon found two blind-cords, which I cut off, and with these I bound his hands all over again, and his feet. Then I searched his pockets and took out everything hard, including a penknife, keys, a cigarette lighter, and an automatic.

I straightened up and stood listening. The silence seemed heavy and menacing. I turned and walked through some curtains into what I realized was the hall proper, a large marble area with doors opening off it on two sides and a window on the third. Sprawled beneath the window was James, and I went over to see how badly he was hurt. He was already coming round, and as I bent over him he started groaning. As far as I could see he had simply been hit hard on the jaw and had given his head a knock when he landed. Being a very tough person, he was soon on his feet, leaning against me and holding his head.

"Did you get the blighter?" he asked. I said I had. "Good; he must have heard me as I entered the room. I had waited quite a long time inside the window and finally decided to explore. But I must have made some noise, and he heard it, because the next thing I knew was that that door opened and he came at me. Unfortunately I was fishing out my torch, and only one hand was free."

"Is there anyone else in the flat?" I asked.

"I don't know, Doctor; we had better explore. Get out your gun," he said, pulling out his own.

I pulled out my small automatic and looked at James to see if he felt fit enough to move about.

"You wait here," I said. "I'll have a look round first."

Ahead of me was the open door; the room beyond it was in darkness. I had not even had time to find the switches before I was aware of the sickly and familiar smell of blood. I expected to find a man—or a woman—sprawled on the floor. But when I had reached the light switches and turned them on, I must confess I was rather taken aback.

I was in a great wide room furnished in opulent bad taste. The floor had its good original tiles, but the walls were hung alternately with grandiose pictures and tapestries. Strewn round the room were heavy decorative furniture of every kind, and execrable sculptures. It was, in fact, like a Victorian stage set for *Othello*. And mingling with the smell of blood was the odour of musk, which I detest.

In the centre of the room was a heavy and elaborate refectory table with large swelled legs; on it lay Messalina, naked and still. I thought at first that she lay on a crimson cloth; but it was blood. She was stretched out on her back, with her arms bent under her, tightly bound. Her head, framed by its luxuriant black hair, lay slightly on one side as if she were tired. It had been severed from her body.

I heard a movement behind me and turned. James Montgomery was sinking into a red upholstered chair by the door. As I looked towards him he bent forward and vomited.

I walked slowly towards the table, possessed by one dominant feeling—relief that someone else had killed Messalina. For a minute or two I stood taking in the details of this strange spectacle.

James had risen and come up behind me. We looked down at the weapon that had decapitated Messalina. It was a great shining axe with a long black shaft, and lay, smeared with blood, across her thighs. I recognized it as the axe in a number of the Redel paintings.

"My God," James said. "Forgive me for making such a scene. I think I'm getting a hold on myself now. But it's that blood that finished me—just look at it, all over the place, and just like a river on the floor." His eyes followed it towards the tall curtained windows.

"There, James," I said, "is Helga Bamberg, alias Messalina, and alias the 'real Redel.'"

"What on earth do you mean?"

"I was a fool not to have realized it earlier. My unconscious has known for a long time, but its message only got through to me just now as I waited outside on the stairway."

"What message?"

"You remember the Redel picture of Messalina's severed head, held up by the executioner?" He nodded. "I should have realized straight away," I said. "The Paris one was painted in a mirror. There was a subtle but definite change in the features. They were, of course, reversed."

"That means *she* was the pupil of our man Leder."

"Yes; she must have been the Gestapo—or rather the Abwehr—decoy; we will get it out of Redel when he comes to—that is to say, if he knows. But first, James, the photographs."

"My heavens, of course! I had quite forgotten for the moment." He undid his shirt and took a miniature camera out of a specially made belt; next came two flat duralumin cases with four small flashbulbs in each. Out of his pocket he took his torch and a small adapter with a long flex. Within a few minutes he had rigged the apparatus, and I was holding up the torch with its flashbulb. He took seven photographs.

"That all right, do you think, Doctor?" he asked when he had done.

"Fine," I said. "It's odd to think of us two spending so much breath devising ways of making her look dead. She couldn't very well be more dead, or better slaughtered for our purposes. However, thank the heavens it's all over. At least one of the heaviest weights is off my poor mind." This last I had not really intended saying aloud, but James made no comment.

We then examined the rest of the room. At the far end, near one of the large Gothic windows, was the "studio" where she painted her horrific pot-boilers. Along with the usual paraphernalia of the artist was a big mirror and a packed portfolio of architectural photographs which she used for her backgrounds. The easel stood with its back to us, and I walked round to see what she had been working on. To my surprise it was quite a competently painted view of the room we were standing in. The refectory table stood, as it stood now, in the centre, and the huge axe with its pale glinting edge lay carelessly across it. It seemed that Messalina had occasionally painted for her own pleasure.

18

We bent over Redel, and I spoke to him in German. "Are you feeling well enough to talk?"

I half expected a baleful glare, but he just flicked his eyes from one to the other of us and then closed them. "I answer no questions; I do not talk," he said in a tired voice. It sounded like the statement of a man without hope.

"I think you will," said James. "We are not the police, and we do not much mind what we do to you. As it is, there may be no official capital punishment in Italy, but there could easily be such punishment unofficially, and after some unpleasant preliminaries. It would be stupid of you to try to hold out. Doctor, let's get him into that other room."

Together we carried him into what appeared to be a small dining room and sat him on a chair. I am not very used to taking part in, or even watching, calculated violence. I wondered if James was really capable of it either, despite his opening remarks.

But to my surprise James went up to the man and took him by the throat almost gently, then shook him as if trying to bring down some unwilling apples from a tree. Redel struggled violently at first; then he suddenly went limp and spluttered that he would tell us anything we wanted to know. He did not seem to care much about anything.

It would be tedious to record the actual questions and answers that went to and fro in that dark room. Most of the time he gave clear and concise information about what I asked him. His own real name was Hans Altmann, but he said he had used a number of aliases. He knew Helga Bamberg had at first been with some branch of German Intelligence, but he had no precise details and did not know at what stage of her career she did this work. He also knew that she had become the pupil of a Munich artist named Leder.

"What happened to that artist?" I asked.

For once he showed some reluctance to answer. Then he said simply, "He died."

"You mean she killed him?"

He paused again, as if acting under some peculiar loyalty. Then he returned to his usual tone. "Yes," he said, "she killed him. I only found that out when we had come to Venice. She said that Leder tried to assault her; that she had hit him with some piece of stage property she found by her; and that she killed him by mistake and fled."

This might just be true, I thought, but no one will ever know now.

Redel said he first met Helga when she joined the Gestapo interrogation centre in which he held a position as translator. In civil life he had been a lecturer in French. Helga had become his mistress, or rather had taken him as her lover, to put it more correctly. After the German collapse the two of them managed to reach Venice, where a considerable number of Germans had gone underground. He said he did not know—and I believed him—who the chief Germans were in this "colony." It was Helga who apparently dealt with the senior members.

To get money, Helga started to paint lurid pictures like

194

those she had seen Leder sell so successfully in Munich (which she had trained herself to imitate when a student with him), and then began to deal in drugs as well. She must have ultimately tired of Redel, because she persuaded him to go to Paris and be the front for an expanding drug and picture traffic which the Germans in Venice were developing through her and others.

As we had thought, it was Joubert who had mentioned our visit and shown Redel some of our horror photographs, apparently in order to persuade him to go into similar production on his own. Redel had sensed something suspicious about our interest and had immediately informed Helga, thinking it was the drug aspect in which we were interested. He also said that Joubert mentioned some connection we had with the Paris police. I must have been unwittingly responsible for that. It had happened when I was speaking to the policeman we called in after our unsuccessful attack on Joubert. I had given Claudel as a reference, and Joubert had, of course, heard.

Helga came to Paris in a hurry, obviously alive to the dangers of the situation, and arranged to meet Redel on the Ile Saint-Louis. He said that she had been friendly and even solicitous, had pumped him of everything he knew or suspected about us. She had stood there talking to him, apparently as one friend to another. Then she had drawn his attention to a barge on the river. Immediately there had been a violent pain in his shoulder. But he must have been turning just as she struck. Not knowing how badly he was injured, nor whether Helga might pull a gun on him, he let himself drop into the water—there is no railing there—intent only upon getting out of her reach.

When he realized, in hospital, that his wound was not serious, and when the police so readily accepted his fake story, he planned to bolt. Having been told by a nurse that the newspapers had presumed his death, he realized he could take his revenge at leisure, and it was now only his revenge that he thought of. As he said to us with scathing bitterness, "I had always trusted her implicitly, as one German should trust another."

Being German, and probably a sentimentalist, he had decided that his revenge should be staged to represent one of her own paintings. When questioned about this, he said he did not know why he had done such a thing, except that he had just had an overpowering impulse to kill her as he did. The symbolism could not have been available to his conscious mind, but it would be clear to anyone who considered his frail person, his ultimate rejection by a woman like Helga, and her attempt to murder him.

He had been supplied with various passports by the Germans in Venice, and he had good contacts in case he had to disappear suddenly. So he first went to a friend's house in Paris, where he kept all his papers; then took the train to Brussels, where he rested until he was ready to travel to Venice.

He knew every inch of the Palazzo Colletta—in which we now were—and he had been able to plan his revenge with care and accuracy. I asked him why he had tried the door handle of Helga's flat, and he said she sometimes left it open if she was expecting any of her contacts. The lock, apparently, was inclined to be noisy.

Once inside the flat, it had been simple. He had gone straight to her bedroom and given her a blow on the head with the butt of his gun, while she lay asleep. He dared not savour his triumph and confront her when she was awake, as she was physically more than a match for him. Then he had stripped her and bound her arms, before dragging her out to the great room, where he had had considerable difficulty in lifting the heavy body onto the table.

"I took some minutes doing that," he added almost apologetically, "because, you see, I am not very strong. I had to get her first into a chair, which I put beside the table, and then stand on the table and haul her onto it beside me."

The rest was soon done. He had found the axe in the "studio" and finished his work.

Redel all of a sudden looked defiantly from James to me, and leaned forward. "I am glad I did it," he said with a slightly hysterical edge to his voice. "I'm very, very glad I did it. Now you can do what you like to me." And the light went out of his eyes as he slumped back in the chair.

So there we sat, this odd trio, in the silence of a Venetian palace in the dead of night, with a sharp awareness of the other member of the company lying there so near to us. I asked myself what on earth we were to do with Redel; the decision had to be made in the light of my plans for Caroline.

"Come outside a moment, James," I said, leading the way into the hall. "I think the only thing to do is to telephone the police and tell them that we picked up the trail of a man we knew to be involved with the drug traffic and followed him here, only to find he had committed a murder." I paused. "You are probably wondering why I don't suggest we ring them and then leave, or not ring them and just leave."

James nodded.

"Well, I must now tell you another part of the story. I think Sir George would not mind, in the circumstances. You see, James, there is a patient of mine—she is at present on Lake Garda—who was one of Cayley's agents and was caught when serving with the French Resistance. It was Helga Bamberg who tortured her during the interrogation and of whom she has been terrified ever since. It is for her benefit that I wanted those photographs—to prove to her, even if it were not now true, that Messalina is dead."

"But how did she know Helga was alive?"

"She never actually knew. But she saw one of Helga's paintings, and also someone in London who resembled her. Although she knows it may be irrational, she cannot help feeling the terror. It is a long story, but the point of it is that, although photographs might have had to suffice if there had been nothing else, the best way to bring Helga's death home to her now would be to show her the body. The photographs will be a useful standby."

"Show her the body?" he cried in amazement. "Do you mean as it is now?"

"No, no. But if we wait here for the police and tell them our story, we can also tell them that we know of someone who can positively identify the body when it is in the morgue. They have already been hunting for the drug contacts here and ought to be quite pleased to have confirmation of who she is."

So that is what we did. James's Italian was better than mine, so he telephoned the report. He had then to ring one of our senior people in Venice—whom neither of us had seen, or ever was to see—to inform him that a woman had been killed in the Palazzo Colletta, and that important documentary leads to the German colony might be available to an expert searcher. That job was not for us. All we had to do was tell them and forget about it.

James rang off and turned to me. "Well, that's that," he said. "Our people seemed pleased, and the police quite mildly excited."

We went back to where Redel was sitting. He still looked gloomy and resigned, but sullen.

"Who are you people?" he said to us bitterly as we came up to him.

"You have asked that before," I said. "As you have done your best for us, I don't mind your knowing now. We are from the narcotics section of the British police. We picked up your trail in Paris." He nodded, but said nothing.

"Herr Altmann," I said after a minute or two, "you don't seem to me a naturally vicious character. How did you get on in that interrogation centre? It was not particularly pleasant, was it?"

"You mean the torturing, I suppose?" he asked. I nodded. He seemed to be lost in his own memories. Finally he said in a tired voice, "No, that was not pleasant; but I did not have to see much of it. I was working chiefly on the translation of French documents. As I told you, I was a lecturer in French at Munich. You may not believe me when I say it was not pleasant. But it is true."

"I believe you," I said. "But tell me, did you ever happen to see or hear of an Englishwoman who was caught with the Maquis—her code-name was Giselle?"

He looked up at me without lifting his head. "Oh yes," he said almost in a whisper, and again, "Oh yes—I remember her. Anyone there at the time would remember her."

"What do you mean when you say that?"

"It was that she-devil who worked on her." He nodded his head slowly towards the other room. "But I did not know it at the time. In any case, I was bewitched by Helga. I had occasion to go into the question room to get some papers. It was during lunchtime, and no one was there—except Fräulein Giselle."

I felt myself going cold, as if a chill wind were blowing through the Palazzo Colletta. "And?" I asked.

"They had not even bothered to lock the door. This Fräulein Giselle was lying there on the floor with blood all over her hands. She seemed only to be able to move her head, and I thought she was trying to speak. But her lips were very swollen, you see, and it was difficult to hear her. So I bent down and gave her a little schnapps from a flask I always carried." He paused. "I shouldn't have done that, you understand. They would have been furious if they had found out. But we all knew about Fräulein Giselle.* She was brave. She should have been a German."

"And did you hear anything she said?" He must have realized the change in my voice. I hoped he would be rewarded in the hereafter for that drink of schnapps.

"I remember the words perfectly, but I do not know what they referred to. She said, 'Father, forgive them.' Do you know what she meant?" he asked.

"It is a quotation from a book," I said, "but you probably wouldn't have read it."

"Probably not," he answered listlessly. "It was a pity she had to die."

---

* Caroline told me that she had chosen the name "Giselle" after the title of one of her favourite ballets.

Down in the courtyard there were sounds of approaching footsteps. The police had made good time. I turned back to Redel—I could not help thinking of him by that name.

"She did not die," I said. "She is alive, but ill. You won't know what I am talking about, but it is quite possible you have helped to get her better."

"Oh, you mean the schnapps?"

"No, Herr Altmann, I do not mean the schnapps; but it doesn't matter for the moment."

19

The arrival of the police was a relief to both of us. The tension began relaxing. When I opened the front door to let them in I was glad to see one of the inspectors we had been introduced to when we had reported our arrival in Venice. He seemed pleased too, and shook our hands warmly before introducing us to his two assistants.

"Ah, Signori," he said, "so you got a line on our birds. Which one has been murdered, and by whom?"

"It is a woman," I said, "and we think we know who she is. The murderer is our friend Redel we told you about—he is in there." And we led the way through the curtains and into the room beyond.

"Ah, so it is he, is it?" He stood with hands on hips, looking down at the melancholy German.

"He says his real name is Hans Altmann," said James. "The murdered woman is in the adjoining room."

The Inspector marched stiffly into the great room, and when I turned on the lights he gave a little gasp. *"Madonna mia!"* he exclaimed. "What a sight! It is just like a melodrama."

"Her name, Inspector, is—I believe—Helga Bamberg. She was the artist all the time—the artist we told you about who put the drugs between the canvas and the lining of the pictures. We followed Redel here, and before we could summon you we came upon this scene. I think I can get you a more certain identification of her tomorrow."

"But why—why this macabre stage-management?" he asked as he walked to the refectory table and looked down at the dead woman.

"She tried to murder Redel in Paris," I answered, "because she was afraid we were on to her drug route and that Redel would squeal if caught. This is his revenge."

"So," said the Inspector in a kind of sing-song, still looking at the body. "She is quite a beauty this one—fine breasts, fine belly." He turned to us. "But, Signori, we must get on with the job, as you would say."

So James and I left the three of them to their routine, and walked out onto the stairway. We lit cigarettes and sat on the balustrade looking at the stars.

"I suppose our anonymous people in Venice will find ways and means of getting in here," said James. "They must have police contacts and all. I also hope they get a lead on the bigger boys in the spy or drug racket."

"Yes, so do I; but thank goodness we don't have that job on our hands as well."

After what seemed an interminable period, the Inspector came out, and I offered him a cigarette.

"Well," he said, "some more of our people ought to be here in a minute or two. They will do the necessary photography and fingerprinting, and then take away the murderer and the murdered." He paused and drew in a lungful of smoke. "Signori, you mentioned an identification. Can you please explain who the witness is?"

"Surely," I said, "but I shall need your help, Inspector. It is at the moment a question of telephoning."

"Telephoning?" he asked.

"Yes. The witness is a lady—Miss Caroline Norton, who is a patient of mine and is at present staying with friends on Lake Garda. If you could have the call made urgent, we could ring her hostess, Mrs. Langley, from the police station and, I imagine, get through quite quickly."

"That is easy, Signor. So let us go, and I will do everything I can to hurry up the connection. Meanwhile I will leave my two assistants here to take care of the rest of the proceedings."

So we left the Palazzo Colletta and walked back through the silent passages of Venice to the Central Police Station. There seemed something incongruous about an efficient police organization in the middle of such an ancient city. One could more readily understand there being an excellent assassination agency here, with every facility for disposing of bodies.

We sat in the brightly lit office in comfortable easy chairs, overcome by a sharp reaction of weariness now that our nightmare was over.

"Inspector," I said, "may I ask you to arrange the identification in rather a special way? You see, the lady in question, Mademoiselle Norton, is still under my care."

"What has the Signor in mind? I shall certainly do whatever I can to help."

"I would like you, if you would, to clean up the body we found and have it laid out in the morgue, quite naked, and with the head well separated from the trunk. That is to show at a first glance that she is truly dead."

The Inspector had been knitting his brows during this recital of mine. "Could the Signor perhaps explain a little why he desires these rather strange preparations?"

I told him briefly that Caroline had been captured when working with the Resistance, and that the murdered woman was almost certainly the German who had tortured her in prison—and had also been recently involved in the drug traffic. "Miss Norton," I concluded, "might be very frightened unless she sees straight away that her torturer—if indeed it be she—is dead. In fact I want deliberately to dramatize the situation."

I was not at all sure that this half-true explanation would appeal to him; but he was a very friendly person and obviously willing to help us. He nodded and said, "I think I see what you intend. It shall certainly be done."

James and I soon became quite fond of this busy-looking and efficient little man. He did everything he could to make us comfortable, and even provided wine and sandwiches while we waited. And his mixture of Italian and English, which I make no effort to transcribe, was quite endearing.

The telephone rang, and the Inspector handed me the receiver. Nellie's voice came clearly over the wire.

"Yes, Harvey, what on earth is the matter? Are you in trouble? Are you still in Venice?" She sounded very worried.

"No, Nellie, I'm not in trouble, but I am in Venice. Be an angel, now, and listen carefully. A lot may depend on what I'm going to say; and I am unblushingly imposing on you for Caroline's sake. I want you to get her and Anne out of bed and dressed, and then drive them here."

"Of course I will, Harvey, but what shall I tell Caroline?"

"Tell her simply that a very important event has happened here which may make all the difference to her health, and that it is vital she come immediately. She may or may not guess what it is all about. But I am certain she will come."

"Where shall we meet you?"

"Let's see, now; it is close on a hundred miles. Say three-quarters of an hour for the preliminaries and four hours for the journey, at the outside. We will meet you in the Autorimessa here at six-thirty. Can you manage that, my dear?"

"Of course I can. It sounds awfully exciting—or isn't it? But don't bother to talk now. *Wiederschauen,* Harvey!"

James and I arranged with the Inspector to meet the car, and we went back to the hotel to lie down. We had asked the Inspector to ring the hotel at a quarter to six just in case we went too soundly off to sleep. I do not know where James's mind wandered before he slept, but mine was following Nellie as she woke up the two girls, and as she explained to George that I wanted the three of them to set off in the small hours of the morning and tear along the deserted roads to Venice. Then I returned to Caroline and watched her in my mind's eye as she obeyed the summons and sat in the car wondering what would be awaiting her at the end of the journey. Finally I think I prayed.

James and I met downstairs in the hotel at six, and just as we were about to leave a smartly uniformed young policeman came through the doors. He surprised both the porters and ourselves by saying in good English that the Inspector presented his compliments and hoped we would make use of one of the police launches.

So, followed by the curious eyes of the hotel staff, we stepped into a smart white motor launch and set off at a leisurely pace up the Grand Canal. We sat listlessly in the launch, watching the bow-waves wash against the ancient palaces and splash round the faded *pali* as they thrust up from the water in their oddly drunken attitudes.

When we drew in to the landing stage by the Piazzale Roma we saw the Inspector standing there ready to greet us. As I shook his hand I thanked him profusely for his thoughtfulness and said—which was indeed true—that such kindness made all the difference in the world when one was engaged on such a gloomy and unpleasant business.

We walked up the steps and over to the great concrete and glass building, the Autorimessa, where every motoring visitor to Venice must leave his car, and which provides him as well with food, information, hotel data, and petrol for his journey back.

We settled ourselves in the central arrival hall and prepared for a long wait. But less than a quarter of an hour later the familiar car appeared at the end of the platform and came slowly along the almost deserted ramp to where we stood.

Nellie, as usual, looked fresh and alert as she leaned out and greeted me. I opened the rear door and smiled at the two girls. Anne seemed either excited or otherwise on edge; Caroline looked up at me with a curious expression I could only interpret as a mixture of hope, apprehension, and trust. She must have sensed that I was making a dangerous throw in the game for her sake, but I hoped she did not also perceive the doubts and fears that possessed me.

Anne and Caroline got out, and I introduced them to the Inspector and James, while Nellie drove off to spiral up four floors where she had been allotted a berth. As this operation, and her return by lift, would take quite a time, I took the others into the restaurant and we all had some brandy. At last Nellie came in, drank up the glass I had kept for her, and said she was ready. So we set off on one of the most unpleasant journeys I have ever taken.

"You lead the way, Inspector," I said.

James walked with the Inspector, Anne with Nellie, and Caroline with me, behind. She took my arm, and we walked in silence. After a few minutes, during which I was oddly conscious of the click-clack of her heels on the stone passageways, she turned her head to me and said quietly, "Paul, I don't know quite where we are going or why, although I feel it has something to do with 'her.' But I want you to know that I realize you are doing this for me, whatever it is, and I trust you absolutely. I hope one day that you will know my gratitude—whatever happens today." She looked down at the pavement and repeated, "Whatever happens."

"I hope, my dear, that because of today you will rediscover your own life and happiness. Look at that gull up there—I am going to take him as a good omen."

We were just crossing a small piazza, and high in the air rode a gleaming white gull, soaring at its ease. A few minutes later the Inspector stopped in front of a severe but oddly elegant building, blotchy with faded pink plaster.

I said, "James, will you look after Mrs. Langley? It is probably best to wait out here in the sun. We shan't be long."

I remember Nellie's giving me a little worried smile as the two girls and I followed the Inspector into the morgue. We walked down a whitewashed passage, past a solitary oleograph of the Holy Family, and came to a stop outside a freshly painted blue door. The Inspector motioned us to wait

208

and disappeared inside. A minute later the door opened, and he beckoned us in. I took Caroline gently by the arm and glanced at her. She looked now almost triumphant, as if she realized that victory was in sight.

Inside the room was a tall white screen. We walked round it and came face to face with what we had come to see. On a shining porcelain table lay Messalina. She lay there almost as we had seen her in the Palazzo Colletta, but now in the pallid rigidity of a recumbent effigy, with the arms stretched close to her sides. Her head lay some six inches from the body.

I did not immediately look at Caroline, but I could feel the tensing of her body as if a current ran through her limbs and was even charging my own hand and arm. Then I turned my head a little and glanced at her. Her eyes seemed to be moving slowly and deliberately over the body; there was little expression in her face, except a certain intentness.

"Caroline," I said at last, "who is that woman?"

"Helga Bamberg," she said quietly.

The Inspector caught the name and gave a little sigh of satisfaction.

Caroline's arm dragged a little on mine, and she seemed to want to move. We found ourselves slowly walking round the table, Caroline's eyes, as before, moving over the head and trunk of the dead woman.

I remained taut with hope and fear until an inane recollection came mercifully to my aid; I was a small boy on the stage of Maskelyne and Devant's in Portland Place, and was walking round the lady who had been cut in half by the conjuror.

After we had circled Messalina it was Caroline again who seemed to take the lead. She drew me towards the door, and I beckoned to Anne with my eyes. We walked out into the passage and along to the main entrance, by which we had entered. I could not make out what Caroline was feeling. Her face was still a mask, but the eyes looked a little feverish.

Outside, Nellie started to raise her hands in a spontaneous gesture of sympathy, and then drew back. As if in a funereal dream we walked away from the building and back along the route we had come. No one spoke, and the only difference I felt in Caroline after we had walked for about ten minutes was that she seemed to be leaning on me a little, and her lovely face was drawn with fatigue. But the feverish look had gone out of her eyes, and for some reason I began to feel an uncertain confidence. I scarcely dared breathe lest my hopes should be exhaled with the air.

"Caroline, my dear, would you like to rest for a while? It's rather a long way to the car."

"No, thank you, I would rather go on. Are we motoring straight back to the villa?"

"We'll do whatever you like."

"I think I would like to go back, if it is all right with you and Nellie." She paused. "Paul, would it be asking too much for you to come back with us?"

"Of course I will come, if I shan't be in the way." For the first time she looked at me and gave a faint smile.

When we reached the Autorimessa the noise and bustle of the arrival-and-departure hall was bewildering. But Nellie secured the car in a few minutes, and we were soon ready to be off, Anne sitting in front, and Caroline behind with me. She was quiet and listless and looked worn out.

I turned to James and the Inspector. "James," I said, "I shall take Caroline back to Garda, so will you send on my things?" I smiled at the Inspector and thanked him for all he had done.

"You may want me for the inquiry," I added, "and I will drive in whenever you say."

He thanked me and added, "I hope the experience was not too much of a shock for Signorina Norton. It was most useful for us to have her confirmation."

I assured him that she would quickly get over it, and idly wondered what the good man would think if he knew how great and transforming a shock I hoped it would prove.

We said our good-byes and started down the ramp and out into a glorious flood of natural light. Soon we were running smoothly down the long viaduct to Mestre, and as I looked back at the sunlit towers and glowing roofs of Venice, I decided with thankfulness that the city I loved so much had not been spoiled for me by Messalina. And if her effect on Caroline worked out as I hoped it might, there would be an added memory of triumph to embellish it.

We did not talk, beyond a desultory remark or two, and were soon through the toll-gate at Mestre. Here starts the smooth and monotonous *autostrada* which cuts straight across the plains for twelve miles, almost to the gates of Padua. We were about five miles along it when Caroline broke down. I had expected it earlier, but was relieved enough when it came. She just put her hands to her face and burst into tears. I inwardly blessed Nellie and Anne when neither of them so much as glanced round, or even ceased the quiet but animated conversation they were carrying on.

As Caroline was shaken by wave after wave of sobs, each wave increasing in intensity, I put my arm round her. At the touch of my hand on her shoulder she did not stiffen as I feared she might. Instead she leaned towards me and buried her face on my chest, her soft hair tickling my nose and cheeks.

It was not long before she was asleep in my arms. She lay there, utterly exhausted, for a full hour, sometimes slowly opening her eyes if a particularly loud lorry passed us, and then slowly shutting them.

We were halfway to Vicenza before she fully woke up and asked where we were. After I told her I asked her if she would like to stop for lunch at San Vigilio, a place I knew she loved.

"That would be nice," she answered, then added, "I'm afraid you've had to prop me up for a long time. I feel much better now." She leaned back in her seat and looked out of the window, at the same time gently putting her hand over mine. I took it and held it without saying anything; nor did she look round. I think she was still a little shy at having to lean, even symbolically, on me.

Two hours later, having stopped for petrol at Verona, we were approaching San Vigilio.

We drove the car to the end of the narrow approach road and parked it on the side; then walked down to the toy harbour, where a few rowboats were tied up. We hired a boat, and Anne and I rowed, the other two sitting in the stern. We pulled slowly out to look at what is one of the quietly classic views of Europe—the little promontory of weathered sunlit buildings standing out into the blue lake, with the perfectly proportioned cypress trees rising behind and above it, like a gently protecting screen.

As we drifted lazily offshore, I had a good look at my patient. I thought there could be no doubt of it; something in her expression, despite her tiredness, showed firm and confident. It was too early yet to assess the result of the shock, but I believed at last we had won.

We ate a light lunch at the hotel by the harbour and then set off for the villa. As we drove home along the shore of the lake, Caroline talked quietly, but in quite a lively way, about the views and the places we passed. We all felt as if a dread malaise had lifted from us, and the result was—speaking for myself—a certain degree of lightheadedness. It all still seemed a little too good to be true, but my level of anxiety had fallen to a luxuriously low point.

After dinner at the villa I told Caroline I should like her to go to bed early with a strong sleeping draught. "I want you to have one absolutely oblivious night," I said, "after the experience you had today—a night which will help to rest you and make you fit enough to assess your feelings tomorrow." We stood on her balcony, overlooking the lake. The water lay below us, sparkling in the afternoon sun, and the soft wind was ruffling the surface along towards Riva.

"Paul," she said, "I want to tell you now. I believe at last it is all over. I can scarcely believe what has happened, but I think I knew as soon as I saw her. She was so finally, so ruthlessly, dead, that I felt the darkness lifting even as I looked at her. But when you are in such despair as I was it takes a lot even to permit oneself to hope—let alone believe

—the end is in sight." She paused and looked round at me openly and frankly, but still—I was glad to see—with that little ducking movement of the head I was always to associate so affectionately with her.

"Paul, did you feel you were running a serious risk in taking me to see her?"

"Yes, Caroline, I did feel I was; but the risk had to be taken. You see, the chance would never have come again, and I had to weigh the probabilities of success against the misery you might have suffered if I didn't risk it. So I went ahead."

"I am not going to thank you now," she said. "I could not think of the right words at present; and they will have to be the very best words I can find."

"Thank you even for those words, my dear. They are reward enough on their own," I answered.

We walked in from the balcony. "Try and relax and let yourself go, Caroline. I will ask Anne to come up and give you the sleeping stuff later on."

As I opened the door to go downstairs she raised her hand in a little salute—or was it a benediction?

When I saw her next day I was certain Caroline was cured. She was tired, of course, and would need looking after for a time, in the good old-fashioned sense. But she was at last free. When she came down to the bathing place at midday anyone could see it in her face and in the way she moved. It is hard to avoid the hackneyed words on such an occasion; when the Langleys, Anne, and myself looked up to see Caroline walking down the steps, I am sure only one word came to the mind of each of us—the word "radiant."

It was Nellie who spoke first. "Darling, you *do* look so

well; come and sit here and be lazy. None of us has bathed today; we just can't be bothered."

Caroline laughed and came across to us, finding a place on the Li-lo between Nellie and Anne. We just sat there and gossiped happily till Bianca sounded the lunch gong.

Postscript

I stayed on at the villa for a week, writing my reports for George Cayley, making quite certain that Caroline was, in aeronautical terms, "powered, sustained, and controlled in free flight"; settling with James Montgomery for him to be present at the Messalina inquiry and at Redel's trial—from both of which I was excused; and at other times lazing about the villa, taking walks, boating, and watching the others bathe.

I had ample time to examine my feelings for Caroline and to deal with them. If that sounds rather cold-blooded, I can only say that I realized with added force the impossible position we all would be in if I tried to intensify the bond between us. My admiration and affection for her ran very deep. Furthermore, she seemed to welcome these sentiments and even return them. But beyond, there was no fair prospect, and I became even glad that we could part with what we had, firmly shared, without danger of painful complications.

So I settled my affairs at the villa and said my adieux to Caroline, Anne, and the Langleys. Anne and I were due back in Wimpole Street in a fortnight, and she was to stay on till then. So I took myself off for my self-promised holiday of escape—the escape from which I benefited most—to the mountains. My destination was a little resort called Flims, in Switzerland, which sits high above the upper Rhine, in its own private valley. There I walked the mountains, sat for quiet hours gazing up at their towering peaks, rode in the "aerial" chair-lift across the lower green slopes, up through the pines, over the rocky wastes, and on up to the eyrie on the Naraus Alp; or drifted on the calm water of the Caumasee, surrounded by its tree-covered walls of rock. By the light of a little torch I read till midnight on the balcony of my hotel room, with its view towards the Ischingelhörner and the curtain of stars beyond.

After I returned to London I heard, almost with indifference, that Redel had been sentenced to eight years' imprisonment—the great provocation he had to kill Messalina being the explanation of the short term; and that Joubert in Paris had been given five years for drug trafficking.

Of the success, if any, that our people had in tracing the German agents in Venice, I never asked and I never heard. It was not in my sphere. But George Cayley seemed so pleased about the outcome of the Messalina case in general that I had an idea there must have been a *bonne bouche* beyond the success with Caroline.

About her he was as nearly jubilant as ever I saw him. But he was quite ruthless about the work to be done, and she was packed off to France in time for the Resistance reunion to which Cayley attached such importance. He never told me the result of it, but he was certainly pleased.

I was summoned to Whitehall one day in the following spring to do a job for him, and I happened to say in passing, "How is Caroline?"

He smiled and said rather abstractedly, "Oh, very well, very well indeed. The Messalina investment paid off handsomely all round, I'm glad to say. I think we shall retire her soon. For, you know, Paul, that miracle you worked on her— or she worked on herself—was not only able to carry her through our work with flying colours; she seems even to be showing some interest in Newcomen. Or so her parents say."